The Something in the Attic

by
B. Payton-Settles

B. Peyton Settles

"Maybe we should pull over," Kiki Moore ventured. "Wait for the truck to catch up."

Mrs. Emily Moore hunched forward, her hands tight on the steering wheel. It looked like hard work, steering the car through blinding rain. The pock-marked road probably didn't make it any easier; it belonged on the surface of the moon. And, as if that wasn't enough, there were no road signs to tell you where you were. This was a job for a man, not someone's pretty brown-eyed mother.

"Hush, Kiki. Don't be a worrywart. I've driven in lots worse weather than this."

Kiki sighed. It would be a first when someone actually listened to her. "Does the sun ever come out in Napa County? I mean, even in San Francisco it didn't rain this much."

Thirteen-year-old Kiki, all elbows and knees, was crammed into the loaded back seat of the family Ford. She pushed boxes and sacks around, trying get comfortable while her sixteen-year-old sister, Joan, sat in the front seat making finger curls with her hair.

"I believe what you said, Mama. Our new ranch will be all roses and sunshine." Kiki balanced her paper dolls on cardboard boxes while she imagined an alternate, happy reality.

Mrs. Moore moaned, "Where the dickens is the road?"

The car lumbered over something hollow. The sound of rushing water and thumping tires came through the rain's rat-a-tat-tat.

"We're going over a bridge, girls. It must be the one at our property line. We're almost there!"

The thumping stopped, replaced by the crunch of tires on gravel. Kiki cleared a spot on the foggy side window with her fist. A brown and white, big-eyed face looked in at her.

"Oh, my gosh! That's a cow!" Mrs. Moore shrieked.

The car inched past the forlorn, dripping animal.

1

"Well, we're definitely in the country." Mrs. Moore laughed nervously.

With a scornful sniff, Joan began to make lipstick kisses on the window. A curtain of rain closed around the cow.

"We don't have cattle on our new place, do we?"

Mrs. Moore glanced at Kiki in the rear view mirror. "No. It must be from the next ranch over."

Shadowy trees appeared through the rain, sodden gray sentinels lining the road on either side. The branches looked like arms raised in damp warning. Kiki leaned over the front seat to peer out the windshield and saw the watery shape of buildings, just visible in the distance.

"Is that it? Right up there." She thrust an arm past her mother's face.

A small white cottage stood there, huddled with other buildings. With its eaves dripping and window shades at half-mast, it could have been crying.

"That's it," Mrs. Moore whispered. Her shoulders slumped.

"Are you sure?" Joan made a face. "Please, Mama, can we go back home to San Francisco?"

"This is home," Mrs. Moore snapped. "Or, it will be when our stuff gets here. You know how lucky we were to find it. Do you really want to go back to that one room we rented from Mrs. Vanderweil? I, for one, got sick and tired of listening to her brag about doing her part for the war effort."

Kiki chimed in, "Yeah, Joan. There's a war on, you know. Be mad at the Germans, not Mama and Daddy." She wondered why their father had chosen this dreary place—he was going overseas soon and they'd be here without him.

Joan muttered, "Smarty pants."

The girls' mother rolled down her window, shouting over the wind. "There's an abandoned house right next to our place. See?"

A tall, narrow structure, mostly rotten gray shingles and

crooked windows, leaned toward the cottage like a monstrous warden.

Joan's face became animated for the first time in hours. "Have you ever seen anything so ugly? It reminds me of the haunted house in that movie I saw last week."

"Your father says it has character." Mrs. Moore flashed them a rare grin.

She parked the car beside the cottage's tacked-on front porch. "No point in getting out yet; I don't have the house key."

Within minutes a truck lumbered up the road through the drizzle.

"Here they come!" Kiki yelled.

With a nod from her mother, Kiki climbed out of the car and dashed to the front porch to wait for the truck. She peeked around the corner at the other house; to her dismay, that building's two front windows seemed to be staring back. She pulled her head in, turtle-style, and hopped from foot to foot—there'd been no bathroom breaks from San Francisco to Napa. She thought about Joan's remark. The old house felt eerie, as if it was hiding something.

Col. Moore stepped out of the truck and moved quickly to the cottage, taking the porch steps two at a time to join Kiki by the front door. When he turned the key in the lock, a bright smile lit up his sun-weathered face.

"Bathroom's toward the back of the house," he said. "Might be a little dirty, but it should work."

"Okay. Hey, Daddy, is that other house ours, too? The one that looks haunted?"

The smile left Col. Moore's face. He glanced toward Fred and Jim, just climbing out of the truck, and gave Kiki a warning glare. She snapped her mouth shut and ran inside.

The living room had the look of a place vacated, but not cleaned up. The floors were scattered with litter and dust balls, and fly-specked windows flanked a grimy oil-burning stove against one wall.

The kitchen, seen from across a threadbare rug and through a doorway, was equally drab. The linoleum on the floor was worn through to its black underside, and the walls were dirty. Mrs. Moore's sparkling white enamel Sears stove, delivered the day before, stood awkwardly to one side.

Kiki tiptoed to the other side of the kitchen, thinking surely this dump couldn't be their new home. It was barely livable, especially compared to the stately, well-kept places they'd admired at the Presidio in San Francisco.

When she heard a creak at the far end of the kitchen where a shadowed doorway led into the depths of the house, the hair rose on her arms. She shook her head: no need to be afraid—it was just an empty, dirty house.

From the front porch she heard her father say, "Looks like this rain's about done, boys. Let's get that stuff inside."

While the men wrestled furniture and boxes, the girls and Mrs. Moore unloaded the car. After a few minutes Kiki begged, "The rain's letting up, Mama. Can we go exploring?"

"Maybe later." Mrs. Moore squinted at the sky. "Right now, grab an armload. And stay out of the way!"

With their arms full of boxes, the girls threaded a path up the steps and moved gingerly through the living room. Joan whispered, "This is creepy!"

Kiki nodded. Luckily their father, right behind them, didn't hear the comment. He was busy talking the place up to his army buddies.

On the way back for another armload, Kiki looked again at the other house, then at her mother's backside—the only part sticking out of the car. "Does anybody live there?"

Mrs. Moore looked over her shoulder. "Oh, no; it's been a burned-out shell for years. After the fire, the people just built a new house next to it." She gave Kiki a brief smile. "Grab the end of this carton."

"I don't like it," Kiki said, lifting the box. "It feels weird—

like it doesn't want us here."

Joan took one end of the box. "This whole place gives me the shivers, Mama. It's cold and creepy."

"Don't let your father hear you say that. He spent our whole savings on this ranch." Mrs. Moore's voice was barely audible.

Chapter Two

The next few weeks were a blur of muddy floors and luke-warm meals eaten perched at the table next to the buckled linoleum counter. Col. Moore served relentless enthusiasm for dessert.

Fred and Jim came almost every day to help them with painting and repairs. When Joan began flirting with the handsome enlisted men, Mrs. Moore sent both girls outside. "They don't need the distraction."

Joan kicked at a rock and then gave her sister a tight smile. "Hey, Kiki, let's go explore the old house."

"You know I don't want to go in there. It'll be just like the tank house and the sheds—dirty." Kiki turned away. "If you want to see the inside so bad, go ahead. I'm gonna go look for squirrels."

"You scaredy-cat! It's just an empty building." Joan flounced away.

Kiki groaned and ran after her sister, yelling, "Hey, knucklehead, wait for me. If I'm coming, I'm sticking to you like glue."

The old house had two entrances, one in front and one at the back. The steps in front were little more than a pile of rotting wood, and the door looked stuck shut. The girls walked around to the back; the door on that wall was at ground level, but the doorknob turned uselessly at their touch.

Kiki relaxed. "Guess we can't go in after all."

Joan smirked, "You wish. We'll stand on a box and climb in through the front."

After making a face at her sister, Kiki followed her around the building's far side. Along this windowless, two-story wall the sounds of life from the cottage were blocked, so the buzzing of insects punctuated an eerie, isolated silence. Even Joan must have noticed, because she picked up her pace to the front corner. When they got there she glanced at Kiki, chortling, "What a baby!" But she looked relieved.

With Kiki close behind, Joan turned the front door-knob and pushed. The door opened suddenly; both girls lost their balance and stumbled. With self-conscious giggles they climbed back up, hesitating at the dark, almost cave-like interior. It reeked of animal droppings—bad news for Joan's new penny-loafers—and the walls were scorched. The top part of a stairway hung from the ceiling.

Kiki pulled in a breath and gagged. "Yuk! What's that awful smell? Do you think somebody kept chickens in here?"

Joan breathed into her sleeve. "I bet it's dead rats. Oh, Kiki, you were right. This is bad."

With her jacket over her nose, Kiki looked at the ceiling. A loosely-woven blanket of cobwebs stretched across the entire room, floating on an updraft. "Shh, Joan." She pointed to the top of the stairway. "Listen!"

A muffled sound, like sobbing, drifted down. Joan took a step back and the floorboard reacted with a loud creak. The sound stopped. With her heart pounding in her ears, Kiki pulled her sister back out the doorway. They tumbled off the box, got to their feet and ran.

The girls tripped on dirt clods, fell, stood up and plunged on. Gradually Kiki's panic subsided. She slowed to a walk and glanced at Joan, who burst out, "What the hell...?"

"Don't swear," Kiki muttered.

They walked for a few minutes before Kiki said, "What do you think that was? That sound, I mean. You heard it, didn't you? Was someone up there?"

Joan shook her shoulders impatiently. "There's no way. The stairs are broken, in case you didn't notice. It was the wind, or maybe branches rubbing the back of the house."

"Should we tell someone, just in case?" Kiki whispered. "Daddy told us not to go in there. We'll get in trouble if he finds out."

"Yeah, you're right." Joan's laugh sounded hollow. "I'll get in trouble, you mean. Nothing is ever YOUR fault."

Kiki jumped right into the familiar, comfortable bickering. "That's not true. I get in trouble plenty."

"Ha." Joan's laugh sounded more like a gulp. "I'm in trouble even when I haven't done anything."

Kiki let the argument go. She knew that whenever Daddy was in a bad mood, Joan got the worst of it. "Joan is in the way," Daddy would growl. "She was born in the way!" He said he was cursed, having only girls; no matter what they did, his daughters couldn't please him.

The girls saw a barn roof above the treetops and walked toward it. This was the Partridge property. Mrs. Partridge had visited Mama yesterday, bringing a pie as a welcoming gift.

Kiki thought about that pie. It was rhubarb, a kind she'd never had before. It was very good. It was also gone. One pie didn't last long in the Moore family. They'd had it for dessert last night, Daddy eating the lion's share after their supper of chipped beef on toast with string beans.

The Partridges' orchard had smoother dirt, no weeds. The girls walked faster. A big house, separated from the rest of the farm by a yard with green grass and colorful flowers, came into view.

A honey-colored bundle of canine energy bounded through the trees, wagging the stump of a tail. When they knelt to pet it, the dog's white teeth sparkled behind a floppy pink tongue.

"Well, hello, boy. What's your name?" Joan returned the dog's smile with one of her own.

While Kiki was fending off doggy kisses, a woman came to the back gate. With her neatly pinned gray hair and housedress, she looked like some lucky person's grandmother.

"Sparky," the woman called. "Come here!" She stepped through the gate and walked toward them. "Hello, girls. I'm your neighbor, Lou Partridge. My goodness, you resemble your mother!" She paused. "Should you be wandering around out here by yourselves?"

Kiki was puzzled by the woman's question. "Oh, we're fine, ma'am. We don't usually get lost, if that's what you mean."

The woman's faded blue eyes looked sharply at the girls. She said, more softly, "I see you've already met Sparky." To the dog she said, "Come, boy, you're bothering these young ladies."

Kiki knew Joan wouldn't let that pass. Her sister loved animals and befriended them every chance she got. Sure enough, Joan spoke up. "Oh, he's no bother. We love dogs. Don't we, Kiki?"

Kiki nodded, pushing Sparky away to keep him from slobbering in her ear.

Joan went on, "Are you Mrs. Partridge?"

The woman smiled. "Yes. Welcome to the valley, girls. It's so good to have a family nearby—especially on the Herschfeldt ranch." The smile left her face. "There's been no one but adults there for ever so long." She looked through the orchard toward the Moores' new home, giving her shoulders an odd little shake. "I hope you'll be happy there. Oh, by the way, everyone calls me Aunt Lou, and Mr. Partridge is just Uncle Harry."

Kiki rubbed Sparky's belly as he lay on his back, tongue lolling out. She looked up eagerly when Mrs. Partridge said, "If you girls can spare the time, there's more of that rhubarb pie in the pantry just waiting to be eaten."

"Thank you, ma'am, but we're not hungry," Joan replied politely.

Kiki, who was hungry and, in her opinion, had not gotten her fair share of the pie last night, nudged her sister sharply.

"Well," Joan amended, with a glance at Kiki, "maybe a little piece would be okay."

The corner of Aunt Lou's mouth twitched. "I can tell we're going to get along just fine. Let's go, girls. And Sparky, come."

An hour later, full of pie, Kiki gawked at the Partridges' lovely old house. There was a separate room just for washing dishes, a special butler's pass-through into the dining room, a piano in the parlor, and a hall closet full of old board games.

"Whose games are these?"

That must have been the wrong thing to say. Aunt Lou ignored the question, saying, instead, "The piano is still in tune, though it hasn't been used much the past few years."

Kiki noticed a hall off the parlor. It had a stale, musty odor, like that part of the house was never used. "Aunt Lou, do you and Uncle Harry have any kids?"

Kiki wasn't sure it was okay to ask, but those empty rooms didn't make much sense. She added, to soften her question, "This would be a wonderful house for a family."

Aunt Lou laid down her dishtowel, lips tightly together.

Joan gave her sister a sharp look. "Don't mind Miss Nosy Britches, Aunt Lou. She's always sniffing around in things that aren't her business."

The old lady glanced away for a second before looking back at the girls. "Let's talk about you kids. Tell me, is it exciting, moving all over the country with your handsome officer-dad? Your mother says you've lived in six houses since you were born, Joan. Why, I've only moved once in my entire life, and that was just across town when I married Harry."

Kiki laughed. "Yep, Mama says she has packing down to a science. Every move is a new adventure, she says."

Joan, diligently combing the dog's silky coat, said, "It's been hard on Daddy, having a family to take care of when he's trying to get ahead in the Army. Mama says we can't get in the way of his career." After a quick glance at the clock above the kitchen table, she jumped up. "Oh, gosh. Mama has no idea where we are. We better get going."

They ran out the back door and down the steps with Aunt Lou calling after them, "Come back soon, girls. And be sure to stay together when you're out exploring."

Halfway across the orchard, the Moores' ranch buildings came into view. The disreputable shell of the old house sat stoically beside the newer one, matching the cottage's glowing windows one-for-one with its drab panes.

Joan turned to look at Kiki's happy, pie-stained face. Her expression erased the younger girl's smile, leaving a pink-framed frown. "You forgot about that horrible old place, didn't you? Well, the fun at the Partridges' didn't just cancel it out. Things aren't like that, Kiki. This is real life, not one of your paper-doll adventures."

Kiki stuck out her lower lip. "I hardly ever play with paper dolls any more. You're not the only one who's growing up."

Chapter Three

That evening, when Kiki and Joan were squabbling over whose turn it was to wash the dishes, their mother took a moment from wiping down her new stove. "Don't they have a lovely place, girls? Mr. and Mrs. Partridge, I mean?"

Joan launched into a thorough detailing of Kiki's bad manners. "And she even asked if they have any kids, Mama. I thought for sure Aunt Lou was going to cry."

"Well, it's a natural question," Kiki countered. "Do they, Mama?"

Mrs. Moore looked thoughtful. "According to what Uncle Harry told your dad, they had a daughter, but she's gone. It was a long time ago, and not something they like to talk about. So, please don't mention it again." She paused. "Oh, that reminds me. What did you get into? I saw you running across the orchard like there was a bogeyman on your heels."

Joan tossed Kiki a quick glance. "We were racing. You know I'm trying out for track in school, Mama. I'm way faster than she is."

"Don't worry, Kiki," Mrs. Moore laughed. "You'll be fast, too, when you grow into those feet."

Later, organizing her thoughts for bedtime prayers, Kiki sneaked a glance at her mother's tired face. She thought about asking God to make the old house vanish during the night, but figured that would bring too many questions. She wondered if God would mind telling her where the Partridges' daughter went.

****

At lunch recess the next day, Kiki's new friend, Leslie, hooked her arm through Kiki's. "I guess you've heard the rumors, huh? I mean, your folks don't care, huh?" She took a bite of cupcake. "If the story is true, it happened so long ago it doesn't matter now."

Kiki tried to cover her surprise. "Oh, yeah." She leaned

against the school's brick wall. "They know all about the story. It's no big deal."

In class that afternoon, while old Miss Tate droned on about algebra, Kiki considered Leslie's comment. If there was a story, she'd better find out about it, maybe talk it over with Joan—not Mama, if it was something bad. She couldn't talk to Daddy, of course. He'd get mad and tell her she was stupid for bringing it up.

The school day finally ended. Leslie was climbing into her mother's station wagon when Kiki hurried over.

"Hey, Leslie, wait up."

Leslie turned, looking back at Kiki.

"You know that story you mentioned—the one about my family's new place? I've heard some of it, of course, but what have you heard? I mean, maybe you know something I don't."

Leslie's mother, with a perfectly made-up frown under dyed brown curls, cut in, "She can't talk now, dear. We're off to the dentist. Get in, Leslie. You know I don't like to keep people waiting."

Leslie gave her new friend an apologetic half-smile, climbed into the back seat, and slammed the door. She put her head out the window as her mother drove away. "We'll talk tomorrow."

Over homework at the kitchen table that evening, Kiki leaned toward Joan, speaking softly. "Hey, Joan, have you heard any stories about this place? I mean, from your friends at school?"

Joan looked up from her math book. "Kiki, don't be so dumb. My friends have better things to talk about than this creepy old ranch."

Kiki rose to the bait. In a much louder voice, she sang out, "Like what? What do big ol' sophomores talk about, any-way? Oh, wait a sec—I know—boys, clothes, boys, clothes, and boys." She laughed so hard she fell off the chair.

Joan looked down at her sister on the kitchen floor.

"That's not all we talk about. And so what if we do, you little creep?" She turned her head to call, "Mama! Kiki's keeping me from studying."

The living room radio clicked off right in the middle of *Gabriel Heater and the News.*

Kiki quickly stood up. "Uh, Oh."

Mrs. Moore strode into the kitchen, mad. "Do I have to stand right here so you'll get your homework done, girls? Your father will be home soon—he won't be happy to learn that you fooled around all evening."

Discipline was their father's job and, on the nights when he came home from the Officer's Club smelling of liquor, he was heavy handed with his belt.

Kiki's mood dropped like cement. "Yes, ma'am." She stood up.

With a theatrical sigh, Joan gathered up her homework papers. "I'll finish in the bedroom, Mama."

Kiki closed her binder. "I'm done." She ran to the bathroom, splashed her face with water, and dashed off to bed.

Later, when Joan was rummaging under the pillow for her pajamas, she gave Kiki a forgiving smile. "Don't get too worried about what the kids say at school, okay? All old places have some kind of story, made up or real. I doubt if anything very interesting ever happened in this dump. Someone's just trying to get your goat." She stepped into the pajamas. "And whatever you do, don't let any weird stories get back to Daddy."

Kiki climbed into the bottom bunk and snuggled under her covers. Leslie's words echoed in her mind and, across the room, the old house looked in through the window. Just before she drifted off to sleep, Kiki heard the front door creak open. There was the low murmur of her parents' voices; Joan switched off the bedroom light.

****

At lunch the next day, Leslie offered Kiki a potato chip.

"Sorry I had to leave so fast yesterday. We were late for the dentist. Ugh. I had two fillings."

"Oh, yeah," said Kiki, pretending she'd forgotten about it. "What did you mean when you said our ranch has a story?"

Leslie took a moment to lick salt off her fingers. "Well," she looked around. "It's supposed to have a ghost." She quickly added, "I don't believe it. I heard it from our cleaning lady. Mother says she's an awful gossip."

Kiki stared down at the potato chip, trying to absorb this disturbing news. Their new home wasn't just run-down and ugly—it had a ghost. After a moment she gave Leslie what she hoped was a casual look. "So what? I already knew that." She stood up and ran across the field.

Strolling up the lane toward home that afternoon, Kiki was glad this was the day Joan had band practice after school—she'd have her mother all to herself for a while. As she opened the front door, though, the sound of women's laughter drifted out.

"Hi, Kiki," Mrs. Moore said. She and Aunt Lou were at the kitchen table. "There's fruit in the icebox."

Aunt Lou, her wrinkles arranged in a twinkling smile, said, "It's a long walk home from school, but you don't look any the worse for wear."

Kiki put her books on the table, got the milk bottle from the icebox, and poured herself a glass of milk. After a few minutes of bored listening to recipe talk, she gave up on getting her mother's attention.

"A little black puppy followed me part-way home, Mama, but he ran off when I crossed the bridge. Can I go down to the creek and look for him?"

"Okay, but be back before supper. You have to do your chores and your sister's, too."

"Yes, ma'am." Kiki ran out the back door.

She walked through the orchard to the overgrown creek, kicking dirt clods. If she found the dog, maybe, miraculously,

Mama and Daddy would let her keep him. Her own dog—wouldn't that be wonderful? Joan would be so envious.

Through the brush Kiki saw brown, mossy stones resting beneath shallow water. Berry bushes, water reeds, and dead tree stumps connected to make a sort of leafy, private tunnel. She parted the foliage, stepping into the muddy creek bed. It was a little squishy, but not bad. She moved carefully to avoid water bugs or slimy creatures.

There was no sign of the puppy. She wandered along, hoping to find a frog or maybe, even, a crawdad. While she was bent over feeling for smooth rocks, she heard the clank of a car door shutting. A motor roared. Aunt Lou's voice warbled, "I'll let you know how that meatloaf turns out."

Kiki stepped onto a log to wave at Aunt Lou. When she stepped off, a pile of rocks on the creek bank caught her eye. There, almost hidden by bushes, was a chimney. She climbed up out of the creek to a flat stone area choked with weeds. The chimney—now looking like an old barbecue pit—was in the center, almost covered by a purple-flowered vine. She walked around it, careful not to stumble on the rough stone flooring.

The place reminded Kiki of the enchanted garden in a book she'd read. Here, beyond the rippling creek, the heavy quiet was broken only by the occasional *caw-caw* of a crow in the orchard beyond.

A short path choked with thistles led to a pile of rotting wood. A lizard stood atop one board, sunning itself. It was gone almost before Kiki saw it, but where it had been, something sparkled in the sunlight. She picked up a small stick, poked it into a gap in the wood, and pulled out a black chain. A grimy, round object dangled from it. A necklace!

When Kiki rubbed the object against her sleeve, a spot of silver appeared. She caught her breath. Maybe it was a treasure. It might even be magic, or cursed—she shuddered. The sun, hanging low through the trees, caught her eye. She slipped the necklace in her pocket and ran for home.

"Mama, Mama! Guess what I found—a picnic place down by the creek. Can you come and see?"

Mrs. Moore looked up from her mending. "You don't say! No, it's too late today—maybe tomorrow. Get started on your chores."

****

Saturday morning began with Col. Moore calling from the kitchen, "Rise and shine, girls. We've got work to do. Up and at 'em."

Kiki heard Joan muttering from the top bunk. She jumped down, pulled on coveralls and a shirt, and stumbled toward the door just as it burst open.

Their father stuck his head in, saying, "No goldbricking this morning. We're heading down to that old picnic spot in fifteen minutes."

After powdered eggs and toast with wartime margarine, which tasted just fine to Kiki, Mrs. Moore shooed the girls out the back door. They joined their father in the tool shed, where he outfitted them with gloves and weeding tools before jamming a work cap on his head and striding off toward the creek. His daughters trudged along behind him, balancing hoes and sickles on their shoulders and rubbing the sleep from their eyes.

It was fun, at first, whacking at tall weeds and digging up roots. As the sun got high in the sky, though, and blisters began to form through Kiki's gloves, she wished she'd never found the old picnic area. She looked over at Joan, gently poking a stubby weed with the hoe.

"Hey, Joan," Kiki called. "Can I do the hoeing for a while? I'll let you have the sickle."

Joan looked up. "Daddy," she sang out. "Want me to run up to the house and get us some lemonade? Kiki wants to do the hoeing. I'll chop weeds when I get back."

Col. Moore straightened his back and wiped his sweaty

forehead. He didn't see Joan's smug grin. "Sure. Get the rake while you're at it. You can drag some of this stuff to the brush pile."

Kiki knew when she'd been outsmarted; she stuck her tongue out at her sister and picked up the hoe. When the metal edge of the tool hit rock, there was a loud clang and a shock went up the handle and into her elbow. "Ouch! Why does the ground have to be so hard?"

Col. Moore gave her a withering look. She didn't like working with him by herself. He tended to focus on everything she was doing wrong, and his temper was short.

When Joan returned with the lemonade, Mrs. Moore was with her. "Oh, Bill, this is going to be lovely once we get it cleared. I'm glad we're doing this first, before we fix up the old house. We can invite our friends over for a barbecue."

Kiki choked on her lemonade and looked at Joan, who jerked her thumb toward the creek. With a finger to her lips Joan laid down the sickle, walking quietly toward the water. Kiki followed, hoping their parents wouldn't notice.

"Did you hear that?" hissed Joan when Kiki got close. "Did you know they want to fix up that old wreck?"

"Maybe they're just talking—you know how they do. Calm down. You'll get us both in trouble." Kiki's hand went into the pocket of her coveralls. Her fingers closed around the treasure. "Hey, I forgot to show you what I found the other day. Look at this."

Just as Joan reached out to examine it, their father called, "All right, back to work. Get those butts in gear."

Kiki hastily put the necklace back in her pocket.

After dinner that night she sat on the front steps in the cool of early evening, pushing at her blisters and thinking about what Leslie had said. Could there really be a ghost in the old house?

Across the orchard Uncle Harry's voice drifted through the quiet evening air, calling the cows to be milked.

"That's it," Kiki thought. "I'll go ask him."

Chapter Four

Kiki jumped up, stuck her head inside the screen door, and called, "Mama, can I go watch Uncle Harry milk the cows? Maybe he'll teach me how."

"Okay, but be home before dark."

She ran straight across the orchard to the Partridges' big barn. Just inside, Uncle Harry sat on a stool by a brown Jersey cow, a pail between his feet. There was the 'squirt, squirt,' of milk hitting the metal and the soft brushing of the cow's tail against the wooden stall. When the animal turned to look, Kiki saw the same liquid brown eyes that had startled her mother on their arrival at the ranch.

Uncle Harry looked around. Spotting her, he frowned. "You must be one of the kids from the old Herschfeldt place. I'm surprised no one told you to stay away from me." He stared at her; then his old face softened. "You want a milking lesson?"

"Yes, sir. I heard you from across the orchard."

"'Well, then. Come over here and watch my hands on the teats. Quiet. We don't want to spook the ol' girl."

After a few minutes, Uncle Harry stood up. "Now it's your turn."

Kiki squatted on the milking stool, took a deep breath of the barn's cool, manure-rich smell, and concentrated. She began milking her first cow. *Squeeze, pull, squirt, repeat.*

"Attagirl. I think you're a natural. The last person I saw pick it up this fast was our little Rosalie."

Kiki lost her concentration. Who was little Rosalie? The milk stopped squirting into the bucket. She gave Uncle Harry a sheepish look before focusing again on the cow's bulging udder.

With Uncle Harry watching, Kiki milked. Finally the stream slowed to a trickle; the pail was full, steaming and foamy. At his nod she patted the cow's firm hide and stood up. Harry lifted the pail by its wire handle and turned away, his face shadowed. "Run along home now, kid."

Kiki gulped. "Can I help you feed the chickens? I helped Aunt Lou yesterday, so I know what to do."

He gave her an irritated glance, but nodded. "Go get the feed sack from that bin over there, and meet me at the chicken coop."

As she tossed chicken feed around the yard to the scrambling chickens, Kiki said, as casually as possible, "Rosalie's a pretty name. Is that your daughter?"

Uncle Harry's face darkened, but at least he didn't start to cry like Aunt Lou had.

"That's right. Rosalie June. But she's gone now. We lost her a long time ago. We don't talk about it—to anyone."

Kiki, on the verge of asking how their daughter got lost, saw Aunt Lou watching them from the kitchen door. The old lady waved, calling, "Come in for dessert when you're finished."

Later, sitting at the kitchen table having coconut cake, Uncle Harry said, "It's been a long time since there were kids around here. Try not to get too used to it, Lou."

Aunt Lou frowned. She turned to Kiki. "You and your sister are like a breath of fresh air for us. And your mother, why, it's as if God decided to give me a replacement until my own sweet girl returns."

Kiki choked on her milk. "Where'd she go?"

Uncle Harry's fork clattered to his plate; Aunt Lou's smile faded. No one spoke. The old woman stood up and, with her back to Kiki, said, "I have work to do." The words trembled in the air. "You'd better be getting back home, child. Don't you have chores, Harry?"

****

Kiki, skipping to keep up with Uncle Harry's long legs, said, "I'm sorry, Uncle Harry. I didn't mean to upset anyone. That question just popped out."

His response was a growl. "Don't bring that subject up again, you hear?"

Kiki nodded. On an impulse, she said, "The people who lived in the burned house—were they crazy or something?"

He jerked around. "Where'd you get that fool idea?"

"Well, a girl at school, Leslie Martin, told me there's a ghost in it—and when Joan and I went exploring inside, it felt really creepy."

Harry's eyes flashed. His mouth formed a grim line. "You don't want to be poking around in there. It's not safe. You go in there, you just might not get out in one piece."

Kiki froze. She croaked, "I'm sorry, Uncle Harry. I didn't mean to make you mad."

He glared at her; a crafty expression crossed his face. He leaned back against the fence, jamming his hands in his pockets. "Well, kid, I suppose the best way to shake you off is to satisfy your curiosity." He looked away for a second. "The Hershfeldt place caught fire back in 1928. It happened in the middle of the night, just before Christmas. No one ever figured out how it got started. Jake Hershfeldt moved out right after. It sat empty for years, 'til Mr. and Mrs. Roos came along. They built your house. We never saw much of them, but they were good neighbors; built up the orchards and put in those walnut trees."

"Wonder why they didn't fix up the old house instead of putting another one right next to it?" Kiki said.

"I wouldn't know, but it damn sure had nothing to do with ghosts. Your pa would tan your hide if he knew you were spreading ugly stories like that." Uncle Harry's face was stony. "Now, get along back home."

At his harsh words, Kiki's temper flared. She sprang away without a backward look. As she ran through the orchard, she thought about the small, silver-framed photo on Aunt Lou's kitchen windowsill. It showed Aunt Lou, Uncle Harry, and a girl. The photo was slightly faded, but the girl's impish, happy face was clear.

Later, Kiki took the necklace out of her coveralls and tucked it into the pocket of her pajamas. She climbed into bed and slipped a hand under her pillow, where she kept her emergency flashlight.

As soon as Joan's regular, slightly nasal breathing signaled that she was asleep, Kiki pulled out the locket and switched on the flashlight. She pushed against the locket's tiny metal catch to slide one fingernail into the almost invisible line between top and bottom of the dirt-encrusted oval. Nothing happened. She spit on the catch, pushing wet bubbles along the line. Her fingers rubbed against crusted dirt. She spit again, this time on the tiny hinge at the back of the locket, before rubbing it on her flannel pajamas. With intense, tongue-stuck-out concentration she pushed one thumbnail against the catch while the other pried down into the gap. The catch moved away from the line, just a hair's width. She quickly slid her nail into the space, pushing hard. The locket slowly opened, held together by the minuscule hinge. There, reflecting the light, was a photo of two faces Kiki had just seen a few hours earlier—Aunt Lou and Uncle Harry looked up at her. She closed the locket, put it under her pillow, and pulled up her covers.

The window's lace curtains fluttered as a breeze moved into the room carrying the scent of roses. Although the only rose bush was an ancient one down by the creek, Kiki paid no attention. She reached under the pillow and wrapped her fingers around the locket. When the breeze touched her cheek, her heart clenched with an unspeakable sadness. She fell into a restless sleep.

****

"We'll join the two buildings to make one good-sized house worth a lot more money," Col. Moore said. He stabbed his pencil at the blueprints spread out on the kitchen table. "Course, we're not selling it anytime soon, honey." This last
24

part followed an uneasy look at his wife.

Mrs. Moore's smooth forehead furrowed into a frown. "I know you'll get transferred again, but we'll keep the ranch to come back to, won't we, Bill?"

Col. Moore gave a reassuring nod before looking at his daughters. "You girls will eventually have the second story of the old building all to yourselves. I figure we can get two good-sized bedrooms up there. What do you think of that?" His smile was smug.

Without thinking, Kiki uttered a small groan which she turned into, "Um, Hum," when she felt Joan's kick under the table.

In a hesitant voice Mrs. Moore said, "It looks good on paper, Bill, but I don't know about putting our girls up in a hundred-year-old building that's been set afire and abandoned."

Col. Moore put down his pencil. "Don't worry. When my crew gets finished in there, it'll be just like new." He stood up and walked to the kitchen door. "Let's go take a look."

When Joan moved to follow Daddy outside, Kiki grabbed her mother's sleeve. "Uh, Mama, maybe we shouldn't go in there—it's spooky."

Mrs. Moore, glancing at her husband's disappearing back, shook off Kiki's hand. "Don't talk that kind of nonsense around your father—no matter what. Do you hear me?"

"But, Mama ..."

"Back in Kansas," Mrs. Moore said, "when your father was a child, he got in big trouble for telling tales about seeing ghosts. That's one subject we don't bring up, ever."

Kiki turned away. She stepped outside in time to see her father jumping over the broken threshold and into the old building. From inside, his voice echoed, "Come on in!"

Mrs. Moore moved forward; Joan walked away. "I have to go to the bathroom."

"Me, too!" Kiki dashed after her sister.

A few minutes later, when Mrs. Moore peered in through the back screen door, the girls looked at her sheepishly.

"I'm surprised at you," their mother sniffed. "I would have thought you'd like exploring. There wasn't much to see, though, I must say—a lot of rubbish and burned walls. And oh, how it stinks!"

Kiki and Joan glanced at each other. Kiki said, "Did you hear any funny noises or see anything strange, Mama?"

"I don't want to hear another word about that, Kiki. Your imagination will get us all in trouble. Now get to your chores before I send your father after you."

As they walked to the rabbit hutches, Kiki pulled the locket out of her overalls. "What do you think of this, Joan?"

Joan waited until they were behind the tank house, then lifted the locket by its chain and swung it through the air. "Wow, where'd this come from?"

Kiki grinned. "I found it by the old patio, stuck in some rocks. Open it. Go ahead!"

Making use of her long fingernails, Joan deftly released the catch. When the locket opened, she drew in a breath. "Who lost this—Aunt Lou? That's her in the locket, isn't it?"

Yes. I've been thinking," Kiki whispered. "Did you know Uncle Harry and Aunt Lou had a daughter? Her name was Rosalie June. She disappeared, somehow, and never came back. Maybe the locket belonged to her." She paused. "You don't think I should show it to Aunt Lou, do you? I mean, I found it, so it's mine now."

Joan gave her the withering, older-sister look Kiki knew so well. "If you'd lost your child, wouldn't you want anything that belonged to her? Really, Kiki!"

"Yeah. I guess so. But, Joan, it might upset Aunt Lou again, like that day when I asked if she had any kids."

Joan shrugged. "Do I have to tell Mama about this? Are you going to give that back to the Partridges?"

"All right, all right," Kiki hissed. "I should have known

better than to show it to you." With that, she turned and stalked through the yard toward the orchard.

When she got to the edge of the lane, she sat down on a large rock. Somehow, she didn't feel right about giving up the locket. She was gripped with the feeling that it belonged here, near the old house. And she sure didn't want to run into Uncle Harry again. She stared down the graveled road.

With a swoosh of air and crunching gravel, Col. Moore's truck pulled up beside her. He rolled down the window. "Which chore is this, Kiki? I don't remember assigning you driveway duty. Get back there and give your mother a hand. She's setting up that big ladder."

Kiki stood, brushing off the seat of her pants. "Yes, sir, but I was just going to the Partridges' ranch. I gotta bring them something."

"Well, hop in. I'm going over there myself," Col. Moore said. "You won't get the job done sitting here, looking like you lost your last friend."

The truck rattled down the lane and across the blackberry-choked bridge to the Partridge property. Col. Moore chewed on a cigar, his elbow hanging out the window. He steered with one hand, tuning the truck's radio to jitterbug music with the other. With his dark hair, sunburned skin, and flashy smile, Kiki considered him more handsome than any movie star. He was always grouchy, though, at least on the rare occasions when he was at home. Contact with him usually involved spankings; at those times he didn't seem so handsome.

Col. Moore cut his gaze over to her. "Cat got your tongue? I never saw you so serious." He reached out one hand and gently cuffed her cheek. "You look like you got the world on those skinny shoulders."

Kiki's frown eased a bit. Her thin frame was a gift from his side of the family, and they both knew it. She wondered if she could tell him about the locket.

The truck pulled up at the Partridges' barn. Uncle Harry waved to them from the corral. Col. Moore jumped out, saying to Kiki, "Take care of your business and be ready to go in ten minutes."

Kiki sat there for a moment, sighed, and climbed out. She walked over to Uncle Harry, who stood leaning against the fence. She stared at her feet, one hand in her pocket. Her fingers closed around the treasure, squeezing it in a goodbye hug. Uncle Harry handed her father a tool before glancing at Kiki.

"Are you fixing to learn some carpentry, now that you've mastered milking?" His friendly tone surprised her. She guessed he'd gotten over being mad.

Col. Moore laughed, "Fat chance one of my girls would turn out to be a carpenter, Harry." He turned to Kiki. "Finish up—we gotta get back."

Kiki dug the tarnished chain out of her pocket and held it up to Uncle Harry.

"There's a picture of you and Aunt Lou inside. See? Do you think it belongs to you? I wouldn't want to keep it if it's yours," she added with a hopeful grin.

At first Uncle Harry looked politely disinterested, but when she snapped the old locket open, his eyes widened. He stepped back, sputtering, "What the hell?"

Kiki instinctively leaned toward her father, who reached out a protective arm. Uncle Harry took the chain in one large, weathered hand. Col. Moore looked from him to Kiki, then back. "What is that, Harry? How'd my daughter get it?"

Kiki had an impulse to twist away and run as fast as she could out of the barnyard. Her father's grip on her shoulder tightened.

Uncle Harry pulled a rag out of his pocket, wrapping it around the locket. "I believe our Rosalie June was wearing this when we lost her, Bill. I'd have to ask Lou for sure, but she never took it off, even at bedtime." He looked toward the house. "It's going to be hard on my wife, seeing this. Where in the world did you find it?"

"Near our creek," Kiki stammered. "I didn't mean to, honest. I just saw it stuck between a weed and a rock. Should I put it back?"

Harry said, half to himself, "You found it by the creek on your property? She never went down there. The man who lived there was a mean sort. Once he kicked our dog just for nosing around." He turned away from them. "Lou! Look what this kid found!"

Col. Moore called after him, "Thanks for the use of the socket wrench." He walked Kiki back to the truck. "Hop in."

Chapter Five

Kiki felt her father's eyes on her as she sat huddled against the passenger door. She knew she was in trouble. She'd made a mistake, again.

Col. Moore reached into the ashtray for his cigar. He went through the ritual of putting the cigar in his mouth, pulling out his lighter, and holding the flame to the slimy green stub. When it lit he sucked in, angling his mouth for a smoky exhale. Finally, he glanced at her. "Next time you find some old junk, leave it alone."

She sighed. "I really liked it, Daddy. It was buried treasure. I only gave it to them because Joan said she'd tell if I didn't. She said it wasn't mine, even if I did find it." Kiki put her chin to her chest in a pout.

Col. Moore stared out the windshield, saying nothing. After taking the cigar from his mouth, he said, slowly, "Joan was right."

Kiki looked at him curiously. It wasn't often either of his daughters did something right.

As soon as they got home, Kiki hopped out of the truck.

Col. Moore called after her, "When we have a minute, let's go down to the barbecue. I want to see where you found that thing."

She turned to nod at him, but was stopped by a scream from around the side of the house. Then Joan yelled, "Mama! Mama!"

Col. Moore hopped out of the truck and fairly flew around the cottage to the weedy space by the old house. Kiki ran after him, stopping when she saw him bent over a pile of clothes on the ground. It took a second to realize it was her mother, lying very still. At the top of the ladder, where it leaned against the old house, tattered curtains protruded from one of the windows.

When Col. Moore slipped his hand under his wife's head,

her eyelids flickered. She groaned. "The window was nailed shut, Bill. It opened by itself." Her head rolled back.

"Oh, god, she's delirious! Joan," Col. Moore snapped, "call Harry and Lou. We need them, on the double!"

Joan jumped and ran. Kiki sank to the ground, legs wobbly. Her father tore his eyes away from her mother to growl, "Get up! Go get that blanket off the couch and then clear out the back seat of the car. Now!"

Kiki was off the ground and up the front steps in a flash. She grabbed the couch blanket, threw it over her shoulder and ran back outside. Joan, behind her, called, "They're on their way, Daddy. Do you want a wet cloth for Mama's forehead?"

Col. Moore took the blanket from Kiki's shoulder and nodded to Joan. "Yes. Thanks," he added, gruffly.

Harry and Lou Partridge arrived minutes later; Lou, tight-lipped and pale, ran to kneel by Mrs. Moore. She rested a hand on the colonel's shoulder, looking at the top of the ladder. "Good grief! She fell from up there? I swear, this place is cursed!"

The colonel didn't seem to hear, but Kiki did. She stared at Aunt Lou, then at the old house and the fluttering curtains. She wondered if she should have made her mother believe what she'd heard in there. Was Mama's fall her fault?

"Let's get her into the car, Harry. I'm takin' her to the hospital." Col. Moore sounded grim.

While Lou supported Emily Moore's head, the men locked arms to move her into the back seat of the Ford. When they lifted her, she screamed. At the sound, Joan grabbed Kiki's hand and held on, hard.

When Col. Moore jumped behind the wheel of the car, the girls scrambled to get in, too. The colonel barked, "Stay here. I don't want you in the way."

Aunt Lou drew in a sharp breath, turning to the girls. "Come with me." She paused, looking at Uncle Harry. "Follow him down to the hospital, Harry. Tell him his daughters will be at our place."

****

Joan and Kiki were in the Partridges' dining room, playing a distracted game of Chinese checkers at the big mahogany table, when Uncle Harry called.

"Girls," Aunt Lou called from the kitchen, "She's going to be okay. She broke her leg, and she has a concussion. That's all, thank goodness."

Joan began to cry. Kiki felt her chin trembling, but she was determined to be strong like her mother would have wanted. Aunt Lou came into the room, quickly putting an arm around each girl. "The doctor said she's lucky to be alive. You're lucky, she's lucky!"

At that, both girls giggled. Joan wiped her nose on the back of her hand before accepting a hanky from Aunt Lou, whose own eyes sparkled with moisture. "He told her not to push her luck —no more climbing around on rickety ladders."

Kiki gulped, tasting salty tears.

Later, during lamb stew dinner in the Partridges' kitchen, Col. Moore called. Aunt Lou talked to him for a minute before signaling Joan, who rushed over to grab the receiver.

"Hi, Daddy! How's Mama?" Joan's eager expression dissolved into a sullen pout. "We could miss school for a couple of days. Oh. Yes, sir. Can we come see her tomorrow?" Then, in a flat, quiet voice, "Bye, Daddy."

Aunt Lou cleared her throat. "They're keeping her overnight? Your father will most likely stay with her. You two can be our guests tonight."

Kiki felt instantly better. Maybe they could sleep in one of those unused bedrooms! She could pretend it was really her room, with Joan just visiting.

Uncle Harry put down his fork, turning a stony face to his wife. "They'll need to stay out of my way, Lou. I'm dog-tired and 4:30 comes early." He flashed a resentful look at the girls. "Lou'll have to drive you to school tomorrow."

Joan curled her lips into a phony smile. "Yeah. We'd only get to stay home from school if Mama actually died."

"Joan!" Kiki gasped.

Her sister's smile dissolved. "I … I didn't mean …" she covered her face with her hands.

"It's been a long day," Aunt Lou said. "Let's clear the table and get the dishes done. We'll need to run over to your house for school clothes."

Kiki sat on a corner of the high, four-poster double bed with her legs crossed, watching Joan carefully refolding a day's worth of clothes before laying them precisely in one of the dresser drawers. Kiki's things were stuffed in a paper sack stowed next to the dresser. She wrinkled her nose. "Does it really matter if your panties are folded just so?"

Joan ignored her sister, saying quietly under her breath, "What I wouldn't give to have a room all to myself, permanently!"

Kiki jumped off the bed, went to the hallway door, and peeked out. Sparky lay half in and half out of the kitchen, head on his paws. When she knelt down and clapped her hands he cocked one ear, bounded down the hall and landed in her arms. She rolled over, one elbow up to deflect his tongue. Across the hall the door to another bedroom was open, slightly. Kiki stood up to investigate, but was immediately blocked by Sparky. When she leaned down to push him away he dodged through her legs, tripping her. With an exasperated giggle, she hugged his neck. "You silly puppy! Don't you want me to go in there?"

Aunt Lou stuck her head out of the kitchen, dishtowel in hand. "Is Sparky bothering you girls? Oh, I see." She hurried down the hall to shut the bedroom door. "Sparky knows we stay out of Rosalie June's room." She pulled Kiki to her feet. "It's your bedtime—Joan's, too. It's been a hard day, and there's school tomorrow."

Although the girls shared a bedroom at home, they were

34

not used to sharing a bed. Kiki found that, where her sister was concerned, the word, "sharing," was a joke. As soon as Joan fell asleep, she began to move restlessly around in the bed. Kiki had just begun to relax, listening to the sounds of the house settling for the night, when Joan's legs started a sort of cycling motion under the covers. A minute later, a bony elbow poked Kiki. The floor was looking better and better. She climbed out of bed and lay down on the rug, tugging at a corner of the bedspread. Instantly, her sleeping sister clutched the spread and moaned.

"Let go, Joan!" Kiki whispered.

There was no response, not even a slight loosening of Joan's grip. Kiki sat up. She thought of the bedroom across the hall and the blankets that were probably in there.

The house was quiet. Kiki wasn't sure what time it was, but she knew Aunt Lou and Uncle Harry must be in bed. With one eye on her sister, she tiptoed across the shadowy floorboards. When she turned the doorknob and pulled, there was a heart-wrenching creak. Joan chose that moment to snort, then settled down, breathing softly.

Kiki crept across the wide hallway to the door of the other bedroom. The bare wood floor groaned, but just a little. For once she was glad to be a lightweight.

The door opened silently. She took that as a good omen and slid inside. It was dark. She didn't dare push the light-button on the wall next to the door, so she stood still, waiting for her eyes to adjust. Through the sepia-toned gloom she could just make out a green and gold dressing table and a small chair covered in flowered cloth reminiscent of Kiki's Easter dress. Sitting in the chair, one elbow on the table, was a red-haired girl in an old-fashioned school uniform.

Kiki gasped, her throat suddenly dry. The doorknob felt icy cold. A trembling voice, which she recognized as her own, whispered, "Hello?"

The girl turned toward Kiki, eyes wide. She seemed to

fade, somehow. Then she was gone. Kiki shook her head, yanked at the doorknob, and bolted across the hall. In the other room, Joan snored on.

Back in bed and snuggled close to her sister, Kiki tried to erase the vision of the red-haired girl. Was it her imagination—she knew there were no other guests in the house—or was she dreaming? No, she had definitely been awake. She gave up trying to figure it out and finally fell asleep, going immediately into a nightmare of being chased by her injured mother, whose face was on fire.

In the rush of getting to school the next morning, no one noticed Kiki's darkly shadowed eyes or her unusual quiet. Aunt Lou did look sharply at her when she left her waffles and eggs untouched, but Kiki said quickly, "It was delicious, Aunt Lou. I guess I'm worried about Mama."

Aunt Lou nodded. "Get on out to the car, now." Peering through the open screen door, she commented, "There's electricity in the air—weather's changing."

Thanks to the party lines, the news of Mrs. Moore's fall was all over the valley by the time Kiki got to school. Suddenly her mother was, 'The lady at the Hershfeldt place who almost died falling from a two-story window.' She was a celebrity. Even Miss Tate, who usually peered over her glasses at Kiki as if she'd never seen her before, smiled and patted her shoulder. She still gave Kiki a "D" on the history test, though.

At lunchtime Leslie threw her arms around Kiki, gushing, "Oh, your poor mother! What will you do without her?"

Kiki growled, "Come on, Leslie. She didn't die. She broke her leg and some other thing, that's all. She's comin' home from the hospital today."

"Well, she's still a hero," Leslie called after her. "You can't pretend she's not. And you are, too, because you're her daughter." She paused, giving a long, loud sigh. "My mother never does anything daring like trying to get into a haunted house." She linked her arm through Kiki's, as if some celebrity status

36

might rub off.

"It's not haunted." Kiki shook off Leslie's hand. "There's no such thing as ghosts."

After lunch Kiki sat at her desk, staring at her open textbook. The vision of the night before intruded on her thoughts, and she had a headache from all the chatter about Mama's accident. She wondered how, if the window was nailed shut as her father said, it opened by itself. And what made the ladder fall, if it was secure like Mama said? She couldn't stop thinking about Mama, crumpled on the ground. What if she'd died? When Kiki thought of Aunt Lou, as upset as if Mama was her own daughter, she wondered how the ghost felt about that.

Chapter Six

Kiki heard the chickens before she saw them. A cacophony of clucking and squawking assaulted her as she walked up the lane. Daddy must have forgotten to feed them this morning before going to the base.

She got some feed from the shed and carried it over to the chicken coop. Agitated brown hens ran at her, pushing, pecking and attempting to fly over one another. With one hand shielding her face, Kiki tossed the grain as far as she could. Fowl and grain flew through the air together. As the birds bullied one another to get to the feed, she giggled. They were so silly! She backed out of the pen, locked the gate, and hurried to the rabbit hutches.

Even though they were Joan's 4H project, Mrs. Moore loved the rabbits. She said she'd always wanted one of those soft, pink-eyed creatures when she was a little girl.

Thinking that if Daddy didn't feed the chickens, he probably skipped the rabbits, too, Kiki ran to the kitchen and, moments later, was back in the yard with a bunch of carrots.

Approaching the elevated wooden hutches, she noticed the quiet. This was odd, because they usually resounded with the scuffling and squeaking of the doe's babies. The still raucous chicken pen faded from Kiki's thoughts. Why were the rabbits so quiet? Were they asleep?

The wire door, usually kept latched, hung open. Kiki groaned and peered inside the box-like enclosure, expecting it to be empty. Instead, she saw four mangled, bloody lumps at the rear of the cage—the baby rabbits. The mother rabbit was gone.

Kiki couldn't make sense of this horror. Her whole body began to shake. She collapsed onto the ground, sobbing.

She gradually became aware of the hard dirt beneath her and the ranch's silence, too. Even the chickens, now sated, emitted just the occasional cluck. Off in the distance there was the metallic sound of someone's plough hitting a rock. Here, though, it was eerily quiet. She was alone on the ranch. She swiped at her eyes self-consciously, and stood. After a quick look around, she moved quickly to the house.

At the back door she glanced at the rabbit hutches; something in the dirt next the old house caught her attention—rabbit droppings! She tiptoed across the yard, knelt down to peek under a bush, and saw the flash of pink pads on the bottoms of brown, furry feet.

"Is that you in there, Brownie?" Kiki called. "What happened to your babies? How did you get out?" Then, as an afterthought, "Don't be afraid. I won't hurt you."

She stood up and walked to the rabbit hutch. With a shudder, she stuck her hand in next to the little corpses, pulling out the water dish. If she could lure Brownie out of hiding with water and carrots, she might be able to catch her.

When Kiki crouched down by the bush, she studied the wall behind it. There was a broken board just above the dirt line, and a gap that a medium-sized rabbit could squeeze through. The rabbit was in the old house.

Kiki scowled, stood up, and said one of the colonel's favorite swearwords. She walked around to the front steps of the old place, took a deep breath and jumped up onto the rotted wood.

The phone rang, jarring the silence. With a sigh of relief Kiki turned and ran into the cottage. "Hello!" She panted.

"I'm glad you came straight home," her father's calm voice said. "I want you to feed the animals."

"Oh, Daddy! Something awful ..." Kiki gasped.

"Don't interrupt. I only have a minute."

She closed her mouth. You didn't argue with the colonel when he used that tone, not for any reason.

Col. Moore continued, "... and then walk down to the Barret ranch. They called last night. Mrs. Barret made us a casserole for dinner."

"Yes sir. Can you come home soon, Daddy? The rabbits …" Kiki's voice wavered.

"Whatever it is, handle it before I get home tonight. That's an order." He hung up.

Kiki stared at the receiver, then sank to the floor below the phone. Those dead babies were still out there. What should she do?

The phone rang again. She stood up, slowly. "Hello?"

"Is this Kiki?" It was a woman's voice. "This is Isabel Barret, your neighbor."

"Hi, Mrs. Barret. My dad said you were making supper for us."

Mrs. Barret evidently didn't like Kiki's flat tone, because she sounded less friendly when she said, "Well, Mr. Barret and I were sorry to hear about your mother's fall."

Kiki couldn't think of anything to say, except, maybe, "So were we." She waited for the woman to continue.

"I'd like you to walk down and get the casserole, if you don't mind. It's ready now." Mrs. Barret's tone was definitely huffy.

Kiki, belatedly remembering to be polite, said, "Yes, ma'am. I'll come right now. It was really nice of you to cook us something."

She grabbed an apple out of the icebox and loped down the lane, glad for a reason to forget the murdered rabbits. In a few minutes she was across the bridge and at the Barret ranch. The house, set back a little from the road, was a hulking, gray and white place with a porch across the entire front and a half-circle gravel drive lined with masses of spiky-looking bushes. A large, grizzled dog got stiffly to his feet and huffed down the steps. From inside, Kiki heard a woman's voice call, "Pepper, shush!"

The dog turned, cocking his ears at the front door. Mrs. Barret stepped out. "My, that was fast. Come in, Kiki."

The Barrets were very old by Kiki's standards—they were

at least 50. They didn't have any children, and, unlike the Partridges, had made no effort to befriend their new neighbors. Kiki figured they didn't like kids, or at least not girls.

She came cautiously into the house to stand by the front door. The living room, which felt unlived-in, displayed furniture distinctly lacking in nicks and worn spots. There were crocheted doilies everywhere. It was the kind of place her mother probably dreamed about—not a room where Kiki, personally, could relax.

Mrs. Barret, evidently sizing up the situation, took the girl's arm to guide her into the less hazardous territory of the kitchen. The enticing fragrance of hot cheese and noodles filled the air. Kiki sniffed eagerly, detecting the aroma of chocolate cake, as well. A picnic basket on the table was probably the source of these delightful smells. Had Mrs. Barret packed this for the Moore family? Kiki was suddenly aware of her lack of manners on the phone.

"You must be a wonderful cook, Mrs. Barret, 'cause something in here smells yummy!" she said, shyly.

The old woman's brisk demeanor softened a little. "I don't get many complaints, dear."

Suddenly Kiki's stomach growled. She put her hand on it, embarrassed.

Mrs. Barret smiled. "It's going to be a while until supper time. Could you use a glass of milk and some custard?"

"Yes, ma'am, that would be really nice." Maybe this lady wasn't so bad, after all.

Kiki stood awkwardly in the spotless kitchen, afraid to sit down at the polished table.

"Why don't you go out back and sit on the bench under the arbor?" Mrs. Barret said. "That's the nicest place around, these fall afternoons. I'll bring out a tray and we'll both have a little something."

A few minutes later Kiki was spooning up custard from a small, footed glass dish while Mrs. Barret's hands cradled a teacup. A hummingbird danced in the air, poking at a dying honeysuckle blossom, and Pepper dozed at Mrs. Barret's feet.

Kiki sighed. "It's really nice back here. I wish we had a yard like this."

"That's right," Mrs. Barret mused. "No one has ever bothered to landscape the Hershfeldt place. Maybe your folks will. It took us a while, when we first came here, before we put in anything that wasn't a food crop."

"Have you been here a long time?"

"Yes, we have. My husband took over this spread from his parents when he and I got married. I moved in here as a bride of twenty-two; been here ever since. Matter of fact, back then his family owned the land on the other side of the bridge, too, where you live."

Kiki took another spoonful of custard. She tried to picture Mrs. Barret as a young woman. She couldn't.

"Was there a house on our ranch back then? I mean, where ours is now? The one that burned looks really old." She glanced at the Barrets' aging house. "Oh! Not that there's anything wrong with old houses. I love them." Her words were tumbling over themselves as she tried to fix the awkward remark. She sighed and quit talking.

Mrs. Barret chuckled. "It's okay. I know this place is old. I love it, too. Yes, that sad, burned building has a lot of history. It was once the only house in the valley."

She took a sip of tea. "It was built by Mr. Barret's grandparents, way back when. It stood empty for years after this house was finished, until we sold off that land to Hershfeldt."

Her comfortable smile left for a moment when she said, 'Hershfeldt.' She looked down at her teacup. "It was a sweet house until he moved in. He was such a horrid man." She glanced at Kiki. "I do believe some of his meanness is still there, in the house."

Kiki stared. "I sure hope not. My parents are set on connecting it to the cottage and making one big place for us."

Mrs. Barret folded her hands. When she spoke, her cheeriness sounded artificial. "That reminds me, dear, is your mother coming home tonight?"

Kiki scraped her dish for the last remnants of custard. "I think so. My sister and I might get to stay home from school and take care of her." Her voice cracked as she answered. She managed a crooked smile, but Mrs. Barret didn't smile back.

"How did the accident happen? I heard she was trying to climb through a window."

"I'm not sure, ma'am. My father said she fell opening a window in the old house, but Mama said it was nailed shut."

She looked nervously at Mrs. Barret, wondering if she should tell her about the rabbits. The words tumbled out. "Something else happened, too. When I got home from school today, the rabbit hutch was open. Our mama rabbit's gone and her babies are dead!"

Mrs. Barret's eyes widened. "Oh, my gracious, that's terrible!"

Kiki took a breath. It was a relief to talk about it. "There's a hook on the door, but somehow it came open. You think it was a raccoon?" She paused. "The bunnies were Joan's 4-H project, but we all loved them."

"No, I don't think a raccoon would do that—certainly not in the daytime; they're night creatures." Mrs. Barret looked puzzled. "I wonder what became of the doe rabbit?"

"Oh, I saw her. She's alive, hiding in some bushes. Joan has to find her and clean up the dead babies, too, before our mother comes home from the hospital. Mama was really attached to our rabbits."

Mrs. Barret put down her teacup. "Tell you what. I'll drive you home. We can get things set up for your mother, and maybe I can help with the rabbits." She paused, saying lightly, "Your father won't mind, will he?"

Kiki thought for a minute. Would he mind? Well she didn't. She just wouldn't tell him. "No ma'am, he sure won't!"

****

As Mrs. Barret's old car bounced up the rutted road to the house, Kiki gazed shyly at this new friend. She cleared her throat. "Do you remember when you said the house still has some of Mr. Herschfeldt's meanness? I've never heard of that before. Can it really happen?" The last part came out in a whisper.

Mrs. Barret, concentrating on parking the car, pursed her lips. "I can only tell you what I think, dear." She gave a quick nod. "When people are happy in a place, good energy stays after they've left. When people are scared or angry, that energy stays sometimes, too."

Before Kiki could ask another question, Mrs. Barret said, "Now, let's go in and see what needs doing before your mother gets home."

They were on the top step of the porch when a horn honked a little way down the lane and a car rolled into view.

"It's Mrs. Partridge." Kiki waved.

"Well, what do you know?" Mrs. Barret exclaimed. "Good to see you, Lou—especially here."

When Aunt Lou came up the steps, Kiki gave her a hug. She held the basket up, saying, "Look what Mrs. Barret made for us. We're getting lots of good cookin' from my mother's accident."

Both women laughed. Aunt Lou said, "Kiki, you should be in politics. You do know how to butter people up."

Once inside, Kiki and Mrs. Barret told Aunt Lou about the rabbits.

"Oh, my stars, someone must have left the door unlatched. But, what could have spooked the doe enough to kill her babies?"

"We don't know that she did," Mrs. Barret said. "Something else could have killed them, and she got away."

Kiki sighed. "We shouldn't tell my mom first thing when she gets home. It's gonna really upset her."

Mrs. Barret picked up a dishcloth. "Well, at least tell your father, dear. He needs to know if there's something preying on your livestock." With a sidelong glance at Aunt Lou, she added, "Pretending something hasn't happened doesn't usually work, in the long run."

Aunt Lou gave her a startled look. "Yes, Isabel. But not all of us are immune to pain."

"Humph!" Mrs. Barret handed Kiki a broom. "Sweep the floor, child. I'll tackle these dirty dishes."

"I'll freshen the sheets and towels," Aunt Lou said. "Kiki, where is the linen closet?"

"In the hallway." She looked shyly at the two old ladies. With them helping, the housework was going to be fun.

Before long the table was set, there were fresh towels in the bathroom and Kiki had made a "Welcome Home" sign for the living room.

"Our next job is to round up that rabbit." Mrs. Barret slipped her sweater on. "It shouldn't be out in the open after dark."

Kiki started to protest—the rabbits were Joan's responsibility, after all—but Aunt Lou shushed her, saying, "You're right, Isabel. Where did you last see it, child?"

With Kiki in the lead, they walked outside to the rabbit hutch. When the women saw the pathetic little corpses, they both shook their heads. It was an awful sight, even for the farm wives. After a minute Mrs. Barret turned to Kiki. "Show us where you saw the mother."

They found the telltale droppings by the water dish, but no runaway rabbit.

"She may have gone in that gap," Mrs. Barret said, parting the bushes. "We should look inside the building."

Aunt Lou stared at the ground. When she replied, her words were choked. "I don't think we should do that, Isabel. You know it's not safe in there." She turned to Kiki, saying, "I need to get home. Tell your mother I'll be over tomorrow morning."

Before Kiki could respond, Aunt Lou was hurrying to her car. Mrs. Barret shrugged. "We can take care of this by ourselves."

Not five minutes after Kiki waved goodbye to Aunt Lou and went back to the rabbit hutch, there was the sound of another car rumbling up the lane. A car door slammed and Joan's voice called out, "Thanks for the ride."

Moments later Joan was at the back door, calling, "Are you out here, Kiki? Oh, hello, Mrs. Barret. What are you doing? The house looks nice, Kiki." She stepped out to join them, stared at the rabbit hutch, and screamed.

Kiki rushed over. "It was like this when I got home. Brownie's not dead, though. I saw her. We're trying to get her for you, right now."

Joan pulled away from her sister, looking angry. "What happened? Who did this? What did you do, Kiki?"

Mrs. Barret stepped forward. "Why don't you come with us, Joan? We've tracked Brownie through a hole in the old building. We need to catch her before dark."

"It wasn't me," Kiki protested. "It was like this when I got home!" She lowered her voice. "We'll listen for Daddy's truck, but you know Mama would want us to rescue Brownie."

Joan hesitated, took a quick look at the hutch, and nodded. "Okay. Sorry," she mumbled.

Inside the old building, both girls huddled near Mrs. Barret. She put a hand over her nose against the putrid air and, talking through her fingers, said, "See if you can find where that hole comes out. Maybe back there, under the stairs."

"It's really dark in here," Joan whimpered. "I'll run home for a flashlight."

"No," Mrs. Barret said. "If you leave, you may not come back. Just prop the front door open."

"I'll do it." Kiki peeled herself away from the safety of the little group and bent down to pick up a block of wood. Something soft brushed against her knuckles, and, with a squeak, she jerked her hand away. From the shadows, two wide pink eyes stared up at her.

"Here she is!" Kiki yelled. "Somebody grab her!"

There was a wild scramble, with Joan shrieking, "Get her! Get her!" and Mrs. Barret trying to block the doorway.

Suddenly Joan surged forward, knocking Kiki to her knees. There was the flick of a rabbit tail near the rear wall, and someone yelled, "Over there!"

Joan froze. The rabbit, cornered, curled back its lips to bare a lethal-looking set of choppers. Suddenly it twisted around, gave a mighty hop, and landed on the stairs. In a flash it was up and out of sight above them.

Mrs. Barret sighed. "Let's get out of here, girls. She'll have to come down in her own good time."

Both girls turned toward the door at the same time and stumbled, falling against each other. As they collapsed, Kiki looked at the stairs; there was the red-haired girl, kneeling at the top. Rosalie June, here? It was too much. Kiki shrieked and plunged through the doorway.

****

Outside in the sunshine, Mrs. Barret patted Kiki's hand. "You couldn't have seen the Partridges' daughter, dear. She's been gone a long, long time. You need to relax. You're over-wrought."

"You're going around the bend, I swear!" Joan said.

Mrs. Barret walked back to the cottage with the girls, gave each of them a hug, and climbed into her car. "Just remember, girls, those baby rabbits are not your fault. I'm sure your parents will understand."

"Yeah, right," Joan muttered. "That'd be a first."

For the next hour Joan hovered by the living room window, looking anxious. Kiki tried to concentrate on her spelling words, but her thoughts kept turning from Brownie to the red-haired girl. She wondered if animals could see ghosts.

Every few minutes Joan ran into the kitchen to check the

time.

"They'll be here soon. Don't worry," Kiki said. "Settle down. You're driving me crazy—crazier." Her laugh sounded hollow.

Joan walked to the radio and twisted the knob to switch it on. "Let's not tell Daddy until after dinner, when Mama's in bed. Maybe he won't be so mad, 'cause he'll be worrying about her."

Kiki chewed on a piece of hair hanging down her cheek. "Okay. Maybe you're right; maybe he won't care about the rabbits—he'll be concentrating on getting Mama settled. We can tell her tomorrow, after he goes to work." She paused, then whispered, "Should I tell her about the red-haired girl— the ghost?"

Joan's mouth made a big, red O. "Absolutely do *not* tell Mama about what you saw. Promise? She'll get upset, and then Daddy'll have a fit."

That night, curled up under the covers of her own bed with their mother home, their father in the living room listening to the war news, and Joan snoring in the bunk above her, Kiki whispered her prayers. At the end, after, "God bless Mama, Daddy, and Joan," she hissed, "And God, why on earth did you move us here? I don't think I can take it."

Chapter Seven

The next morning, as Kiki sat at the kitchen table spooning Cream of Wheat into her mouth, the colonel announced, "I'll be taking care of your mother today. You're going to school, Kiki. Hurry up and finish eating." He didn't sound like he wanted an argument.

"Am I staying home, Daddy?" Joan's voice cracked a little. The look she gave Kiki clearly said, *Oh, no—he'll find the rabbits before we have a chance to clean the cage!*

"Yes. I may have to go to the base later." Col. Moore paused, glancing at his younger daughter. "Kiki, go get dressed. Make it fast."

Standing in front of the bedroom mirror while she struggled into a school dress, Kiki looked at her frowning reflection. She picked up the old pig bristle hairbrush, gave the ends of her braids a couple of strokes, and sighed. She was going to have to tell Daddy about the rabbits.

After a quick detour to kiss her mother, Kiki ran to the front door. With one hand on the doorknob she called, "Daddy, something got in the rabbit hutch and killed all the babies. I found them yesterday when I got home from school."

Col. Moore stared at Kiki through the kitchen doorway. A muscle in his jaw twitched. "What in the hell?"

Kiki edged out the door, talking fast. "Mrs. Barret knows about it. She came over to help me. The doe rabbit was hiding in the bushes, but before we could catch her she went through a hole into the old house. We tried to get her, honest! And Joan tried, too, but it got dark and we ran out of time." She sucked in a breath. "I gotta get going. Bye!" She snapped the door shut and ran down the steps.

By the time she got to school, the bravado of her confession was gone. It was a dumb idea, and she'd be getting the worst spanking of her life when she got home. She sat at her desk in the stupefying classroom, where the only sound was the erratic buzzing of a fly. Her father's shocked face kept pushing into her thoughts; she stared out the window, nibbling at her fingernails.

Mrs. Tate's shoes made a rubbery squish, squish across the room. Then, without warning, the scratchy-looking wool of the teacher's skirt came into focus, inches away. Kiki looked up, putting one arm across her blank paper.

"You'll be staying after school, Kiki, if that essay isn't finished."

"I really need to get home right after school, Miss Tate," Kiki whispered.

"Well, then, get busy! No more daydreaming." Miss Tate's gaze shifted to another slacker in the next row.

A girl sitting near Kiki gave a sympathetic sigh. "She's so mean!"

Kiki picked up her pencil. My Favorite Place, she wrote at the top of the lined sheet. Huh—anywhere but here!

When the dismissal bell rang at three o'clock, Kiki was still writing. She gave the teacher her most pathetic look, but Miss Tate simply shook her head and turned away.

When the other students filed out of the room, Leslie stopped near Kiki's desk. "I'll wait for you," she whispered. "My mom's gonna be late. Maybe she'll give you a ride home."

At 3:15 Miss Tate looked up from her work. "It's time to stop, Kiki. Your grade will reflect your effort—or lack of it."

****

"Mom, Kiki had to stay late. Can we give her a ride home, just this once? Please?" Leslie's words came out staccato-style.

Mrs. Martin picked up the cigarette burning in the car's ashtray, took a long drag, and blew out a stream of smoke. She turned to look at Kiki, standing in the open door in her faded cotton dress. With a roll of her eyes, the woman clamped the cigarette between her teeth. "O.K., just this once. We have things to do. Climb in."

52

The girls were both quiet on the ride to the Moores' ranch. Kiki couldn't help but compare Leslie's rude, tough-looking mother to her own Mama. She felt a pang of sympathy for her friend.

When Mrs. Martin's sedan came to a gravel-spewing stop at the Moores' front door, Kiki climbed out, called a polite, "Thank you," to Mrs. Martin, and, louder, "Thanks, Leslie."

Daddy's truck was not there, thank goodness. She stepped into a quiet house—there was no sign of Joan, and Mama lay sleeping in the bedroom with her leg propped on a mountain of pillows.

Kiki tiptoed into the kitchen. Joan, kneeling over something on the back porch, looked up. "Thanks a lot, Benedict Arnold."

"I was trying to take the blame. I thought he wouldn't be so mad at you if he heard it from me, first. When's he coming back?"

"I don't know. He probably won't even spank *you*. He acted like it was all my fault." Joan sounded tired.

"Sorry," Kiki mumbled. She stepped out onto the porch. In an awkward attempt at patting Joan's hand, she bumped against a wooden cage.

"Brownie!" She gasped. The wayward doe rabbit peered up at her through wire mesh.

"I had to go in that awful place and get her by myself," Joan said. "She was sitting next to the door, like she was waiting for me. She even let me pick her up."

"Did – did you see anything?"

"What do you think? There's nothing in there but dust and dirt. You've got to quit imagining stuff, Kiki. We've got enough problems without your wild ideas."

"Now, wait a …"

Joan interrupted. "Mama felt really bad about the babies. She had Daddy set up the cage here, so they can keep an eye on Brownie. Daddy said we can't be trusted any farther than he can throw us." Joan's face, as she turned to go back inside, was tear-stained.

"Kiki, are you out there? Come in and see me." Mrs. Moore was awake.

Kiki ran inside. "Hi, Mama! Are you feeling better? Can I get you anything?"

Her parents' bedroom, a small space filled with heavy furniture, seemed to bulge with fat white pillows.

As she stepped into the room, Kiki heard the sound of a car out front. She cringed; Daddy must be back.

Mama leaned against the cushions, closing her eyes. "That's probably Lou. When she brought over these extra pillows, she said she'd bring us something for supper. Go let her in."

Kiki opened the door, hoping it wasn't her father and his belt. Aunt Lou stood there, carrying a cardboard box emitting the mouth-watering fragrance of ham and sweet potatoes.

"Can I put that in the kitchen for you? Mmm! I can't wait 'til supper."

Aunt Lou smiled. "If you look inside, you'll find a plate of sugar cookies for your afternoon snack. I swear you and Joan are like the granddaughters I should have had!" She looked toward Mama's bedroom. "Is she sleeping? I'll just pop in for a minute."

"Come on in, Lou," Mama called. "I'm making good use of those pillows from your daughter's room. Thank you so much!" This last part was followed by a shrill, whistling wind from between the two buildings.

While Aunt Lou and Mama talked in the bedroom, Kiki and Joan devoured the still-warm cookies. "You have to take that dish back to the Barrets," Joan said.

Kiki gave her sister an insolent grin. "As if I'd trust you alone with these cookies." When she'd eaten the last of her share, she picked up the Barrets' casserole dish and ran out of the house.

A car engine sounded at the end of the lane. Was it Daddy? Should she run and hide in the creek? When the truck nosed around the curve, she relaxed. It wasn't Daddy.

A blustery wind pushed at the trees; Kiki leaned into it, squinting in the dullness of early twilight. She shivered, feeling sorry for the orchard's bare, lichen-covered branches. She wondered if they felt the cold.

In the distance, lights blinked on at the Barret house. She hurried forward, pretending she'd just cleared second base and was making a home run. Pepper barked when she ran up the wooden steps; before she could knock, the front door opened.

"Hi there, Kiki!" Mrs. Barret's face was all smiles, unlike yesterday.

"Here's your dish, Mrs. Barret. And, guess what? We found Brownie. My dad and Joan put her in a cage on our back porch. She'll be safe now."

"Well, thank goodness. I was really worried about her. And how is your mother? I'll be by tomorrow, if she's up to having company."

"Oh, she's fine. She's stuck in bed with a zillion pillows. Aunt Lou brought them from her daughter's room." Kiki thought wistfully about all the pretty things in Rosalie June's bedroom.

Mrs. Barret, reaching into the icebox, turned. "Oh, did she? I'm surprised at that," she said, half to herself. She chuckled. "Lou wasn't very good at sharing – her daughter or her things. Those two did everything together. They even wore matching outfits!" She paused. "Ralph and I were never blessed with a child to indulge."

Kiki nodded. When she spoke, her voice was wistful. "We don't get indulged. There's two of us, and my father wanted boys—or a dog."

Mrs. Barret frowned. "He should appreciate the blessings God gave him, instead of wishing for something else." She looked toward the window and sighed. "You'd best be getting back home; it's almost dark, and I imagine you have home-work."

Kiki turned toward the living room. "I sure do. I have to describe a person out of the story Miss Tate read to us: The lady in, *The Legend of Sleepy Hollow*." She paused before adding, "It's a ghost story. Of course, there's no such thing as ghosts—is there?"

Mrs. Barret looked away. She put a hand on the front doorknob. "That's a whole, big subject for us to talk about some other time. Right now I'll just say that, in the opinion of some very wise people, there's dead, and there's gone, and they're not always one and the same. Now run along home."

Kiki hurried out the front door and down the steps in the semi-dark. She pondered Mrs. Barret's words, realizing that, if someone else believed in ghosts, maybe she wasn't crazy.

****

Col. Moore called to say he'd be home late, which meant Kiki and Joan had their mother to themselves that evening. In spite of the girls' protests, Mrs. Moore got out of bed to sit at the table for dinner.

"I swear, you're fussing over me worse than two moth-er hens!" Mrs. Moore said, irritation in her voice. "Just sit down and eat your dinner, both of you. I want to listen to the news."

While the girls were doing the dishes, their mother brought up the subject of the rabbits. "I know it wasn't your fault, Joan. Your father thinks you were careless, but I'm not so sure. He thinks I was careless with the ladder, too. And I know I wasn't."

Joan stood with her back against the sink, dishes forgot-ten. She reached for a dishtowel, wiping her eyes.

"I really did close that cage door yesterday morning after I fed them, Mama. I remember doing it. And I got in trouble, anyway!"

"Your father will be calmed down when he gets home. He

may still be a little disappointed in you, Kiki, for what you said this morning." Mrs. Moore rested her elbow on the table, her cheek in the palm of her hand. "I doubt if we'll get any more rabbits." She stood up. "Help me get back to bed, will you, Joan? I'm worn out."

As she hobbled out of the kitchen, Mrs. Moore gave Kiki a wan smile. "Sweep up those crumbs, please."

The broom was hardly out of the closet when Kiki heard her mother shriek. She dashed to the bedroom, seeing her mother and Joan huddled in the doorway. A mass of cloth, feathers, and wilted red leaves lay where Aunt Lou's pillows had been, and, behind the bed, a breeze ruffled the curtains.

Mrs. Moore disengaged herself from the girls and hobbled over to the bed, lifting first one pillow, then another. "They're torn, from a knife—or claws! How … What …?"

Joan lifted a pillow by one corner. "Aunt Lou is sure to blame us."

"I don't understand. Did some animal get in from out-side? Wouldn't we have heard it?" Mrs. Moore sagged against the bed.

Kiki walked over to the raised window frame. "It must have crawled in here. Oh, gosh, maybe it's still in the house!"

"We'll just see about that!" Joan grabbed the broom from Kiki, using it like a baseball bat to smack the bedroom's faded wallpaper. "Get out of here, critter!" she shrieked.

Mrs. Moore raised her voice to say, "That's enough, Joan. Put the broom down. Whatever it was, it's gone now."

Joan lowered the broom with an embarrassed smile. "I was just trying to help."

"I think whatever came in through the window popped back out the same way, Mama." Kiki's voice cracked, like it always did when she was scared.

Mrs. Moore brushed her hair back from her face and looked around the room. "You could be right. Nothing came through the kitchen—it must have gone back out the way it came." She squared her shoulders. "The wind must have blown those leaves in here. Maybe that's why there's no animal smell."

Kiki got an armload of torn cloth and feathers. "I'll put this stuff on the back porch for now so you can lay down, Mama. Do you want the couch pillows?"

Much later, when their parents' bedroom was clean and their mother was finally resting, the girls sat at the kitchen table, speaking in whispers.

"That window wasn't open when we got Mama out of bed. I remember hearing the branches scraping against it. Did you go in later and open it?" Joan sounded tired.

"Of course not; why would I? And even if I had, why would I tear up the pillows? How could I somehow do all that while we were eating and doing the dishes? Huh, Joan? Huh?" Kiki heard the panic in her voice. Whatever was going on, it was getting worse, fast.

"Quiet, Kiki." Joan cut her eyes toward the bedroom, where their mother was probably still half-awake. "Okay," she whispered. "What in the world is going on?"

Kiki, words tumbling over one another, told her about seeing Rosalie June's ghost twice—in the Partridges' bedroom and in the old house. She finished with, "Maybe it's jealous of Mama. Maybe it thinks Aunt Lou likes Mama best. There. I've said it. And I'm not crazy!" She stopped talking and slouched back in her chair.

Joan raised one hand. "No more. You're way off base, Kiki. You've been reading too many scary books. You have to stop talking and thinking this way right now. Do you have any idea how mad Daddy would be if he heard you say there's a ghost on our ranch? He loves this place!"

Kiki crossed her arms over her stomach. "Well, what's your explanation?" she said, through clenched teeth. "Will you at least admit someone, or something, is trying to hurt Mama?"

58

She pushed away from the table and marched onto the back porch, slamming the door. From a far corner of her cage Brownie squealed, looking terrified. Kiki dropped to her knees, murmuring, "Sorry, Brownie. I forgot you were out here, or I wouldn't have come through the door like a charging bull."

As she sat with the rabbit, staying very still, familiar evening sounds soothed her—Joan moving around the kitchen, the deep voice of the radio announcer on, *I Love a Mystery*, an owl hooting beyond the sheds. From the chicken yard came clucking sounds; most likely one of the hens was jockeying for position on the roost. Brownie, eyes now closed, snored. Kiki wondered if she was dreaming about her babies. Finally, swiping at her snotty nose with the back of her hand, Kiki stood up. Anger cooled fast without a coat.

Chapter Eight

Kiki didn't want to go back inside, even though it was a freezing night. Joan's words still stung. She thought about running away, but to where? Hmm—she could break the news to Aunt Lou about the pillows. That would help Mama. Grabbing an old work jacket from a hook by the screen door, Kiki went out into the night.

The wind in the orchard was putting on a performance: branches sawed against one another like violins, dead leaves rustled, and bird calls bounced first here, then there. Kiki lowered her chin and made a beeline toward the light shining from the Partridges' kitchen window.

At the back steps, Sparky emerged from the shadows, at first whimpering and then furiously wagging his tail. Kiki petted him and, after a look at her reflection in the window, spit-combed her hair and wiped her face.

The wooden screen door rattled beneath her knock, but there was no answer. She knocked again, this time on the kitchen door. No footsteps sounded on the kitchen linoleum; no voice called out, "Come in!"

Kiki hesitated, then opened the door and stuck her head inside. "Aunt Lou?"

With one hand holding the dog's collar, she took a quick look around the kitchen.

Except for the shadowy corners, it was empty.

"There's no one home, Sparky. Wonder where they are?"

She shut the door, hovering on the steps. The door clicked open again, swinging wide. Sparky stood, a growl low in his throat. Kiki, one foot on the ground and ready to run, croaked, "Who's there?"

Sparky suddenly clamped his teeth onto her sleeve and yanked her back. Girl and dog scrambled out of the yard and across the gravel, not stopping until they got to the barn. Kiki caught her breath, feeling a little silly. She hoped no one had seen them running scared from a kitchen door.

"Is Aunt Lou in the barn, Sparky? Let's have a look."

She pulled the massive wooden door open and slipped inside, breathing in the aroma of hay, manure, and machinery. In the semi-darkness two cows shifted their weight, peacefully chewing their cuds. Their udders were limp, high; they'd been milked. Sparky flopped down, putting a paw on Kiki's foot and closing his eyes. Within a minute he was snoring.

Kiki heard the, 'cluck-cluck-cluck,' of a chicken in the hayloft above. She looked up at the yellow beak and bright eyes of a brown-feathered hen.

"How'd you get up there, Biddy? You belong in the hen house, this time of night. Are you stuck?" She spotted a ladder nailed to the wall near the hayloft and climbed slowly up, murmuring, "It's okay. I won't hurt you."

The hayloft, really just a big shelf built below the barn roof, was dark and musty; Kiki squinted, looking for the hen. She spotted it a few feet away and turned slowly, reaching out a hand. It squawked and flapped its wings, revealing six brown eggs.

"So that's what you're up to! You have a secret nest! Are you hoping to hatch them? This isn't a very good nesting spot. I bet there's rats in this barn."

She lunged toward the chicken; it scrambled to the edge of the loft, spread its wings, and sailed to the barn floor. "Oh, no! Come back here!" Kiki threw herself toward the ladder, her knee knocking hard on something hidden in the hay. "Ouch!"

When she sat back, rubbing her leg, she noticed a dark rectangle sticking out of the straw. Curiosity piqued, she grasped it and pulled. Some sort of book, old and covered in straw dust, popped free of its hiding place. After a hard shake to belch out any black-widow spiders, Kiki gave it a cautionary stomp and slipped it in her pocket.

Taking the ladder rungs two at a time, she jumped down

onto the barn floor. Telltale brown feathers stuck out behind a row of shovels. "Here, chick-chick-chick. You need to get back to the hen house, with or without those eggs."

With quick hands Kiki scooped up the little bird, called to Sparky, and ran across the barnyard. She boosted the hen into the chicken coop, gave Sparky a pat on the head, and turned toward home.

The farm's night sounds settled around her; the snuffling of livestock, the thunk of a gate against its latch, the plunk of a drop of water into the watering trough. When a cricket sang an experimental note, she wished she could be that cricket, or even the hen now safe on its roost.

As she plodded through the orchard, tree branches reached out thin, gnarled fingers, but Kiki was calm now. They were just trees, pretending at ghostly shapes. As she approached the house, she looked to see if Daddy's truck was out front; it wasn't. She wished he'd hurry home. She knew Mama wouldn't be safe until he returned.

With a lift of her chin she strode into the kitchen. "I know, Joan, I know. I shouldn't have run out in the dark. I'm back now. Please don't tell the folks."

Joan looked up from her homework. "Cripes, can't you just pretend to be normal for a couple of days, until Mama gets better?"

Kiki hung the jacket on its hook before facing her sister. "Is she asleep? I'll rest on their bed until Daddy gets home."

Joan frowned. "Okay with me. It's your funeral. I'd think you'd want to stay as far away from them as possible." She turned back to her books.

Curled up on one corner of her parents' bed, Kiki let herself be lulled by the humming furnace and her mother's soft breathing. Her eyelids drooped. Her head snapped up once before sleep claimed her.

The next thing she knew, a strong hand shook her shoulder. In the darkness, her father's voice whispered, "Kiki, wake up. I'm home. Go back to your own bed."

Kiki opened her eyes. Her fuzzy brain registered her father's exhausted face. With a nod she unfolded and slid off the bed. To her amazement, her father grasped her in an awkward half-hug as she edged around him and out of the room.

It wasn't until she was secure beneath her own covers that she remembered the book. Her sleepy thoughts went to a story Leslie had told her the day before, about a rat who was a king. Maybe the book belonged to that rat. Who else would read in a hayloft? She pulled the blankets up around her ears and went to sleep.

****

"Get up, lazybones! We have to fix breakfast this morning!" Joan sounded grouchy already.

Kiki stretched and winced as her bare feet touched the cold floorboards. "Okay, okay, I'm coming!" She grabbed her clothes and dashed into the bathroom.

Col. Moore's voice came clearly through her parents' closed bedroom door. "Now, be careful, honey. That's right. I've got you. Lean on me." The door opened to Mrs. Moore, coming through on crutches. Kiki smiled, giving her a V for victory.

At the breakfast table a little while later, as the girls spooned up Cream of Wheat, Col. Moore put his coffee mug down and turned a grim face to his daughters. "Your mother is very upset about losing those rabbits. That's two times, now, your carelessness has hurt our family. If you two knuckleheads don't start doing things right, you're going to be sorrier than you've ever been."

Mrs. Moore, looking pale, put a hand on his arm. "Will you help me get back to bed, Bill? I can't sit up any longer."

The girls' father did not look happy at having his lecture interrupted. "Oh, right."

When he turned to lean in close to the girls, eyebrows drawn and black eyes boring into them, they shrunk back.

"Nothing else can happen to upset or hurt your mother. Do you hear me? Nothing. It's up to you girls to take care of things while I'm on maneuvers next week. If I get any bad reports about either of you, there'll be hell to pay!"

With that he took his wife's elbow and guided her out of the room. Kiki stared at his retreating back, her appetite gone. She slid a look at Joan. "Are you staying home with Mama again today?"

"I think so. He's going to the base." Joan's chin trembled.

Kiki nodded. "I'll clean up the kitchen."

"You don't have time. You're almost late. Get going." Tears sparkled on Joan's eyelashes.

"So, I'll be late. So what? If the school calls, you answer the phone. Tell them I was helping at home," Kiki snapped.

When Col. Moore strode into the kitchen in his uniform, hat, and overcoat, Kiki was up to her elbows in dishwater.

"What are you doing? Joan is staying home today, not you. Get your coat. I'll drop you off at school. Now!"

Kiki jumped like a startled deer, dashed to the back porch for the jacket hanging on the hook, and circled round the house to her father's truck. He pushed the passenger door open for her and she climbed in, casting an apologetic look toward the kitchen window.

The five-minute ride to school was tense. Kiki knew her father would have no sympathy for the tears crowding behind her eyelids. She cleared her throat. With her face turned, she stuttered, "Do you really have to go away, Daddy? Do they know you have a family to look after?"

Col. Moore groaned. "Did you forget, Kiki? There's a war on. I have to do my job. Your job is to help your mother while I'm away. End of discussion."

The truck careened onto the school grounds just as the first bell rang. Col. Moore reached across her to wrench the door open, and Kiki jumped out. Before she could say good-bye, he pulled the door shut and gunned the motor. She watched as the truck roared away.

School seemed to go on forever. Kiki ran a daydream in her head every possible minute, but she couldn't avoid the scary thoughts about what might be happening at home. During the spelling test her mind just would not focus—she missed fourteen out of the fifteen words, even though she'd been studying them all week. Miss Tate handed her the "F" paper with a sharp look, and, thank goodness, no comment.

At lunch recess, Kiki dashed to the far end of the playground, hoping to sort out her thoughts alone in the crook of a low-branched tree. She hoisted herself up and reached into her pocket for food. Instead of smooth, cool apple skin, her fingers touched gritty leather—the old book.

She dug into the other pocket for her apple, found it and took a bite, flipping open the book's cover with her free hand. Faded, precise writing showed itself on a yellowed flyleaf:

Happy eighteenth birthday, Rosalie June

Kiki's eyes widened. She took another look at the cover. One word, DIARY, was stamped there.

She quickly finished the apple and opened the book again, turning to the first page. There, inked only a little more precisely than her own scrawl, were sentences written by the living Rosalie June.

The first few pages recorded the daily life of a farm girl thirty years ago. Rosalie June's writing showed little imagination. Kiki was, nevertheless, fascinated with the small details the girl referred to as, "my horribly boring life."

Glancing up, Kiki saw Leslie coming across the yard. She jammed the diary back in her pocket.

"Want some of my lunch?"

Kiki felt a rush of guilt. Leslie was a good friend, and Kiki had barely spoken to her these last few days. "Sure. Thanks."

Leslie climbed into the tree and gave Kiki a deviled egg. "How's your mother today?"

"Not so good. She was really hurt bad."

"Would it help if you came over to my house after school for the next few days? I could ask my mom. And you could see our new foal. She looks just like Star, except she's black, like her daddy." Leslie giggled.

Kiki sighed. "Oh, I wish I could! I can't wait to see her, but I have to help my sister take care of things at home. I won't be going anywhere after school for a while."

Leslie finished her egg. "Do you think maybe I could come there and help you? That would be kind of fun, too."

"Nah," Kiki muttered. "There's not gonna be any fun at our place for a long time."

"It doesn't have to be fun. We're best friends, remember. Or has that changed?" Leslie's face was serious.

This startled Kiki. "Oh, no, Leslie, that hasn't changed. I'm sorry if I've been rude. You're my best friend, I promise!"

Leslie climbed down to the packed dirt ground. "You don't have to say that. I know you've lived in a lot of places; you probably have lots of friends you like better'n me." She started back across the playground.

Kiki jumped to the ground. "Wait, Leslie!"

When she caught up with her, Kiki grabbed Leslie's arm. "Can I tell you something? You've got to promise you won't think I'm crazy, and you can't tell anyone!"

The bell rang. Leslie smiled. "Sure. Meet me in the bathroom in five minutes."

Chapter Nine

"You really think a ghost caused your mother's accident?" There was disbelief in Leslie's voice. Kiki turned away, fists clenched.

"Nobody else believes me, either."

Leslie coughed. "You gotta admit it's pretty strange."

At that moment, Lila Witherspoon's imperious voice burst into the bathroom, echoing off the tiled wall. "Hey! Miss Tate wants you back in class, NOW!"

Kiki and Leslie moved off the cold bathroom wall and sauntered along behind Lila. "Listen," Leslie said, "I think you're being kinda silly. There's no such thing as ghosts."

Kiki felt like she'd been slapped. Her face turned beet-red. Without thinking, she pulled away from Leslie to run past the classroom door and onto the empty playground. As she stumbled through the chain-link gate, unwelcome tears erupted. She moved forward, only dimly aware of the dusty path.

A short distance from the school she stopped, leaning against the gray, bark-peeling trunk of a huge eucalyptus tree. She knew she should go back to school, but she'd be laughed at and in trouble, too. If she went home early, Joan would tattle on her. No matter where she went, she was in trouble.

She sat down, her back against the tree. The eucalyptus, with its' carpet of seedpods and slippery leaves, its' oily fragrance, and its' creaking branches, felt like an old friend. After a few minutes she stood up, moving slowly toward home. Her thoughts turned to the puzzle of the locket, the book, and the red-headed ghost.

A dog's distant barking startled her. She was almost at Barret Lane—she should hide. She saw the tangled blackberry bush at the corner mailbox and climbed behind it, perching on an old fencepost. No one would look for her here. She felt in her pockets for lunch leftovers—no such luck. With a sigh, she pulled out the diary and thumbed through its pages. Most of them were blank—the writing began on the first day of the year and stopped in mid-March. About ten pages from the last entry, Kiki read,

> *Dear Diary,*
> *I finally have something interesting to write. I've made a new friend!*
> *It's a secret, so I can't tell anyone—especially Mother. He said she wouldn't understand about us liking each other, because she doesn't want me to have any fun.*
> *She's coming! More tomorrow.*

The next few pages were entirely about Rosalie June's new friend, 'Mr. Handsome.' She described him in great detail, right down to his cowboy boots and red neckerchief. To Kiki's disgust, the writer said he had, 'the cutest little dimple on his chin.' When she wrote that she guessed she had, 'the teensiest bit of a crush,' Kiki rolled her eyes. It sounded just like Joan, talking about boys. She wondered if it was someone Rosalie June met at school—then she wondered why she called him mister.

Kiki thumbed forward to March 12, the final entry.

> *Dear Diary,*
> *This is the biggest secret I've ever kept from Mother and Daddy.*
> *I know they'll understand, someday. Mr. H. wants me to come to his house tonight after dinner, when they're at Grange.*
> *I am so lucky to have a boyfriend who …*

It ended in mid-sentence. Kiki closed the book, puzzled. Who was Mr. Handsome? She thought about how mad her parents would be if Joan did something like that. It seemed very romantic—just like Romeo and Juliet. But, if Rosalie June and Mr. Handsome ran away together, then how did

Rosalie June get to be a ghost?

The air was growing chilly; mist was settling into the orchards, cocooning the branches. Kiki stood up, pulling her jacket tight around her. It was time to go home while she could still see the ruts marking the road.

She set out, moving fast in the early twilight. After a few minutes there was the faint jingling of bells. Pepper came out of the haze, a furry, four-footed apparition. Kiki couldn't help smiling when he flashed a fanged grin.

"Pepper! What are you doing out here?"

At her delighted laugh the dog bounded forward, planting his forepaws on her shoulders. He managed a wet lick before she pushed him away.

"Down, boy! I'm already soaking wet." Kiki knelt to hug him. "Should you be out here on the road? I better take you home."

She tied her blue scarf to Pepper's collar for a leash, holding one end. After a minute he pulled away and ran on ahead, grinning back at her.

"Do you want me to come home with you?" She shook her head. "That's not such a good idea. I'm an outlaw today. I'll knock on the door for you, but then I have to scoot."

They bounded up the Barrets' front steps. Kiki knocked, told Pepper to "Stay!" and stepped back into the mist. The front door clicked open. Mrs. Barret peered out.

"Why, Pepper! When did you learn to knock? Is someone out there with you?" There was silence, then, "Hmm. That's odd."

Kiki smelled the heavenly fragrances of baked bread and peanut butter cookies before she tiptoed away. Her stomach growled.

Tires crunched on gravel. An engine sounded close by. She hopped to the side of the road, looking for cover as a truck emerged through the mist. Uncle Harry, his surprised face staring through the windshield, braked to a stop.

"Kiki! What the devil are you doing out here? I almost hit you!"

Kiki shrugged and came over to the truck, putting one foot on the running board. She frowned in through the side window.

"Hi, Uncle Harry."

He reached over to push the passenger door open. "Climb in. You're getting soaked. School let out early?"

When she got into the truck she made a big production of closing the door so she wouldn't have to look at him. "No. I didn't feel good. I decided to come home." She wished she didn't have to lie. "You can just drop me off at the bridge. I'll run the rest of the way."

Uncle Harry's caterpillar eyebrows slanted down. "I'm surprised the teacher let you walk home if you're sick."

Kiki studied her hands. "Yeah. Me, too."

"Let's go see what Lou has to say. If you're really sick—and, you don't look it—you probably shouldn't be around your mother."

They drove the short distance to the Partridge ranch in silence. Kiki watched rivulets of moisture run down the side window. As they walked from the truck to the house, she blurted out, "Uncle Harry, do you know how to get rid of a ghost?"

He stopped, looking irritated. "What are you talking about?"

"Well, I saw a ghost at our place and here, too. I need to get rid of it." Her voice trailed off—he probably wouldn't believe her, either.

"What kind of a ghost? What does it look like?"

"Well, it's, it's ..." Kiki's voice came out in a squeak. "It's your daughter, Rosalie June." She cringed.

Uncle Harry's eyes bulged. "How would you know that?"

"I saw the picture on your windowsill. That's who it was."

Uncle Harry's big hand gripped Kiki's shoulder. "Let's

not go inside just yet. Come on over to the barn. We need to talk."

Once inside the barn, Harry leaned heavily against a stall and pointed to an upended fruit crate. "Sit."

When Kiki was perched on the wooden box Harry pulled out a dog-eared tobacco pouch, tamped some pungent flakes into a pipe, and struck a match to light it. Then he squinted at her. "Is it this ghost thing that's making you sick?"

"Yes, sir."

He puffed on his pipe. "Exactly where have you seen it?"

Kiki's head snapped up. Did he believe her? "You really want to know?"

"I'm asking, aren't I?"

She took a deep breath. Here goes nothing, she thought. "It was in one of your front bedrooms—and in the old burnt house, too."

Uncle Harry pulled on the pipe. "Are you telling me you saw the same ghost in two places?"

"Yes, sir, and that's not all." Kiki gulped. "It's trying to hurt my mother."

Uncle Harry set his pipe down. He studied his gnarled fingers. In a curiously flat voice he said, "Seems to me, if there is a ghost," he looked sideways at Kiki, "it should be left alone. You're just gonna get people upset, talkin' crazy like this. I say leave it be. Forget about it." He stood up, his expression cold.

Kiki got to her feet, talking fast. "But what about my mother? She's already hurt, and the ghost might do something else!"

Harry bent to put his face close to hers. "I'll tell you what would really hurt your mother—you running around half-cocked, spreading stories about her new home. Oh, and another thing: Lou still thinks Junie Bug is coming back. I sure don't want you breaking her heart."

He stomped out of the barn. When Kiki darted through,

he yanked the barn door shut. Kiki stood still, uncertain what to do next. Across the yard the Partridges' stately old house no longer looked friendly. She needed to run home, but first she had to ask one more question.

"What exact day did she disappear—Rosalie June, I mean? I know it was a bunch of years ago. Was it March 12th?"

Uncle Harry gagged. "How in the Sam Hill did you know that? Who have you been talking to?"

He was suddenly next to her, grabbing her arm. She twisted away and sprinted into the mist-shrouded orchard, running blindly. After a few minutes she stopped dodging trees and hid behind one. She quieted her breath and listened for the crunch of Harry's boots on the hard dirt. There was no sound. Was he back there?

Off to the right, green branches poked through the gauzy mist. She was near the creek. The damp, gray stones of the barbecue pit loomed among the glistening leaves, the fog draping wispy tendrils around it. In her light corduroy jacket Kiki shivered, thinking about Harry. He said his daughter never came over here; that wasn't true—this was where she'd lost the locket.

"I guess kids don't tell their parents everything when they start growing up," she muttered. "I wonder if Uncle Harry knew about Mr. Handsome?"

Kiki crept toward home. When she jammed cold hands in her pockets, she felt the leather diary. What was the name of the guy who owned our ranch back then, she wondered. Let's see: John—no, Jack. Or was it Jake? Hershey bar. She giggled; Hershfeldt, not Hershey bar; Jake Hershfeldt, initials JH. She gasped, stumbled, almost fell. Oh, no! Was he Mr. Handsome?

"Kiki! Kiki!" Joan's screech seemed eerie, disembodied through the fog. "I know you're out there. Uncle Harry just phoned. You're in big trouble. You better get in here."

Kiki shrugged, thinking, what's new? She tucked her chin into her collar and trudged toward the house, wondering if Uncle Harry had called Mama to tattle on her.

There was the sound of feet on the road behind her, then a familiar jingling sound. She ducked into the bushes, squatting to watch as the misty shapes of a bundled-up person and a dog moved past. They climbed the porch steps and rattled the screen door with a sharp knock. When the door opened, Joan stood, backlit in the living room's cheery light. Her company voice floated across the chilly air.

"Hi, Mrs. Barret. Oh, you brought Pepper! Come on in."

As soon as the door closed, Kiki crept up onto the porch, putting one eye to the keyhole. She couldn't see anything, but warm, doggy breath coming through the keyhole made her blink. She jumped back, bumped against the railing, and tumbled down the steps. She lay on the hard ground for a minute, rubbing scraped elbows before creeping around to peek in through her parents' bedroom window.

Inside, her mother and Mrs. Barret sat on the bed. A glass dessert plate was on the dresser, piled high with cookies. Kiki thought of the aroma from Mrs. Barret's kitchen when she took Pepper home: cookies.

Mrs. Moore's voice came clearly through the curtained glass. She sounded okay—not like someone stalked by a ghost. Joan appeared in the bedroom doorway, carrying teacups. Her hair, usually shiny and coaxed into a flip, hung oily and limp next to her face. She looked tired. Maybe taking care of a sick person wasn't so easy, Kiki thought. Joan hadn't even brushed her precious hair.

When her sister glanced toward the window, Kiki ducked and fell.

"Should I call Kiki, Mama? She's out there somewhere, playing—I just know it," Joan's voice chirped.

Mrs. Barret said, "Oh, that reminds me; I found this scarf on Pepper. Is it Kiki's? I noticed her wearing one like it the other day. Pepper had it tied around his neck when he came inside this afternoon."

Mrs. Moore's voice sounded thin, like it did when she was worried or nervous. "Yes, I believe it is. We got a call from Harry Partridge a little while ago. He gave Kiki a ride up the lane this afternoon. She must have left school early. I'm just waiting for her to come home and explain herself—where is that child, anyway? It'll be dark soon."

"Daddy will have a fit, won't he, Mama?" Joan sounded smug.

Mrs. Barret spoke again. "I know Kiki was worried about you, Emily. She's such a sensitive child; and it was strange, that ladder collapsing like it did."

Mrs. Moore's response echoed Kiki's surprise. "Do you really think she's sensitive? All we notice is her overactive imagination; and Bill has no patience with dreamy little girls right now—there's so much going on at the base. When he finds out she played hooky from school, he'll be livid."

Chapter Ten

Kiki jumped down from the window ledge and stole through the damp, stringy weeds to the backyard. Sheets flapped on the long wire clothesline in a ghostly dance—it was laundry day. While she stood there trying to decide where to hide, the back door opened. Joan emerged, carrying the laundry basket.

"Kiki! There you are. It's about time! Here, help me get the sheets in. We have to hang them inside, over the doors. They're not getting dry out here."

As Kiki slouched across the backyard, her sister reached for a clothespin, gasped and recoiled. "Aaugh! Something's on them—and on me!" Joan's hand was crawling with maggots.

Kiki grabbed the hose to spray water on the rice-like larvae, yelling, "Stand still! I can't get them off while you're flailing around."

A gust of wind threw the water back in Kiki's face and made the sheet billow out like a sail. The clothespins popped open, releasing their grip, and the sheet was airborne. It thumped against the side of the old house, catching in an upstairs window.

"Oh, Kiki, now look what you've done!"

"Me? Me? Why is everything my fault? I didn't put those bugs on the sheets. I didn't make the wind come up! And I didn't make Mama fall off that ladder so you'd have to stay home from your precious high school!" Kiki started to cry.

Joan grabbed the hose to finish washing the maggots off her arm. "Okay, okay. I'm sorry. Be quiet—Mrs. Barret'll hear you. Let's just get that sheet down from there and get back inside. Yecch!" She shivered, clenching her teeth.

"No. I don't want to go in. I'm in trouble—in case you forgot."

Joan groaned. "Be reasonable. You have to come inside sooner or later. Tell you what: I'll go in and tell Mama about the bugs. You get the sheet. When you come inside, she'll be too busy with this mess to think about being mad at you."

Without waiting for Kiki's response, Joan ran inside, calling, "Mama!"

Kiki walked over to the moss-encrusted wall of the abandoned house. From where she stood, the sheet looked like a tissue hanging from a weepy eyehole. She shook herself, thinking, 'What're you crying about, house?'

She drifted past her parents' bedroom window; the women were still talking, but her mother's voice now had a steely sharpness. Kiki ducked and ran to the front yard. The crate—the one she and Joan used in place of steps the first time they went in the old house—sat where they'd left it. She hesitated, wishing the sheet had blown somewhere else—anywhere else. She sighed, hopped up on the box and stood at the threshold of the old building.

The smell of rot dominated the dead interior. She gulped a breath of fresh air, took three quick steps, and stood in the middle of the room. Telling herself, fiercely, that she'd imagined everything about the ghost, Kiki moved toward the stairs. Her head swiveled at a scuttling noise—a mouse ran straight up the wall, disappearing where wall met ceiling. She fought an urge to run back out the front door, telling herself, 'It's a mouse—just a mouse. Stay calm.'

At the stairway she stood on tiptoe, stretching upward. The steps were far above her. With a sigh she ran outside for the crate. Using it as a booster, Kiki grasped the charred planking and swung her legs onto the bottom stair. There was a loud cracking noise. She gulped, held on, and elbowed her way to the next step. With intense concentration, she moved upward. Any outside sounds—a dog barking, voices shouting her name, even a truck engine growling—became part of the effort to hang on and move upward. At last, nose against musty floorboard, Kiki squinted over the top step.

Damp, malodorous air hit her. Fighting the urge to creep

back down, she peered through misty gloom into the cave-like space. She had expected to see a bedroom, maybe with old-fashioned furniture, but this looked like somebody's attic. Open beams draped with spider webs sheltered clusters of what she really hoped were not bats, and furniture was piled in the center.

She made herself focus on the sheet, a white blur against the far wall. She cautiously circled the pile of furniture—it looked a bit like an island—and crossed the room. Each step brought agonized creaks. There was another crack and a foot-sized hole appeared. Kiki fought back panic and tapped the floor in front of her—it held. She shifted her weight and slowly, carefully, moved toward the window.

In the yard below, Mama called her name. Joan, sounding whiny, said, "She was here a minute ago, Mama, honest!"

The back door slammed. Kiki's frustration bounced around the silent attic. What did Joan use for brains, anyway? This mission to rescue the laundry was her idea!

Kiki's hand was on the damp sheet when she heard Mrs. Barret say, "I'll let Pepper off the leash going home. He might catch her scent. Don't worry. She'll turn up."

The lighted windows of the cottage, from Kiki's attic perspective, looked inviting. Home seemed snug and safe, nestled down there. Maybe Leslie's right, she mused. Maybe this ghost idea is silly. She began tugging at the skewered cloth.

Movement on the gravel road caught her eye; Uncle Harry's farm truck—two glaring eyes and a big metal nose—rumbled into view. While she watched, her fingers manipulated the cloth away from the jagged glass. Suddenly, "Ouch!" Blood oozed from Kiki's finger. She put the cut up to her mouth—she'd have to find some other way to free the sheet.

She looked at the furniture: chairs were placed in two rows like soldiers on guard, and lumpy stuffing—probably once a mattress—lay between. There were rags and sticks on the mattress, with an odd-shaped ball at one end. Maybe one of those sticks would work. Without warning, the hairs on the back of Kiki's neck stood up. Eeuw! This place felt so private—was she trespassing?

She edged cautiously to the furniture. Someone, long ago, had strung rope around the chairs. At her touch, it crumbled. She thrust a leg between two chairs and slid her foot under the stuffing.

Something warm and soft brushed her ankle. She screamed, stumbled, and fell face down against the ball. When her eyes opened, the sockets of a human skull stared back.

Terrified, Kiki rolled, pushed up on her hands and knees, and scrambled to the stairs. When a chair crashed to the floor, she glanced over her shoulder—Rosalie June stood next to the bed, mouth open and face contorted in a heart-wrenching wail.

Kiki threw herself at the stair railing, missed, and collided chin-first with the top step. Her head, then her shoulder, banged hard against wood. With the yawning hole directly below her, she reached out to grab the step. At that moment, the ghost's sobbing resounded through the attic. Stars burst inside Kiki's head. Her fingers relaxed, her grip dissolved, and down she went through the darkness.

Chapter Eleven

Voices coming from the yard beyond the building brought Kiki to a dazed awareness. She heard Joan say, "That's where I heard something crash, Mama. I bet she's in there, just like I told you."

"No, Honey. She knows that's off limits. Are you sure you saw her? Maybe she went home from school with one of her friends. I'll call Leslie's house. Help me get back inside." Mama sounded worried.

Kiki tried to yell; her throat didn't work. She willed herself to stand up, unfold from the floor—nothing happened. Her head throbbed, crowding out thought. She lay in a heap, listening as the old building creaked in the wind. The ghost's sobbing had stopped. The heavy downstairs air was quiet. A mouse, perhaps emboldened by the stillness of the form on the floor, scampered over for a nervous sniff. Kiki cringed, but couldn't move—just thinking was agony. The mouse darted away. Kiki lapsed into semi-consciousness. When a hand touched her shoulder she groaned, struggling to open her eyes.

"Kiki! Wake up. It's Dad." Her eyes opened to a blurred vision in green fatigues, an unshaven face, and a sour, sweaty smell—Daddy. She saw the fear in his face dissolve to his usual irritated scowl. "What the hell have you done now?" And then, with a sigh, "Can you move? Where does it hurt?"

Kiki managed a whisper. "I didn't get the sheet."

She tried to lift her head, felt a stabbing pain, lost consciousness again. A moment later she was aware of her father's hands cradling her. He got to his feet, carrying her in his arms.

"Joan, go tell your mother we've got her. Make it snappy. She's hurt."

Joan ran from the room, shoes clattering across the floor. From the cushion of her father's arms, Kiki murmured,

"Sorry, Daddy."

He made a funny, gulping sound and whispered into her ear, "Sorry never saved anyone's bacon, kid."

Behind her father, someone moved. Kiki looked around him and into Uncle Harry's weathered, stony face. When her startled eyes met his, he took a step back. With a tight, humorless smile he said, "Let's get her out of this dump, Bill. It's a goddamn hell hole."

Kiki hid her face in her father's shirtfront on the quick trip across the yard. When he lowered her onto the couch she looked around, hoping Uncle Harry was gone. No such luck. His hulking body filled the doorway.

"Kiki!" Mrs. Moore's voice caught.

"Uh-hum." Uncle Harry cleared his throat. "I hope this taught her a lesson, folks. There's a bogeyman in this valley that don't take to bad children."

The cool hand her mother had placed on Kiki's forehead moved away. Mrs. Moore sat up straight. From deep within the couch pillows, Kiki groaned.

Col. Moore strode across the room to rest one hand on his neighbor's shoulder, his face reflecting bitter exhaustion. "No warning needed, friend. Thanks for letting me know about her nosy behavior and smart mouth. When she recovers from this, she'll answer to my belt."

Tears trickled down Kiki's cheeks. She burrowed into the couch pillow. The front door creaked open, snapped shut. The sound of Uncle Harry's boots on the porch punctuated the parlor's awkward quiet. Kiki's mother spoke, sounding very tired. "What did he tell you, Bill? Was she asking about their private business from years ago?"

Col. Moore nodded, his face stony.

"What possessed her to meddle like that?" Mrs. Moore continued. "And she played hooky from school—what's gotten into her?"

"I know, Emily. The last thing you need, with me going

overseas, is for word to get around the valley that our kids are troublemakers."

Kiki opened her mouth, hoping to plead with them. She felt Joan's hand on her shoulder. From the corner of her eye she saw her sister's whispered, "Not now."

Mrs. Moore hobbled out of the room, leaning heavily on her husband's arm.

From the kitchen, Kiki heard the sounds of dinner being readied. When she heard Joan say, "I'll do Kiki's chores, Mama, until she gets well," she groaned. So this was what shame felt like.

A bit later, while Joan fed her a spoonful of soup, Kiki whispered, "There's something horrible in that attic, Joan. I saw it."

Joan put her nose right next to Kiki's, hissing, "Stop this craziness right now. Don't ever talk about that stuff again. Don't even think about it. Didn't you hear Uncle Harry? Do you want to end up being the, 'something horrible,' in the attic? For heaven's sake, Kiki, you're not much, but you're the only sister I've got." Joan's straight, tight-lipped mouth was just like their mother's.

Col. Moore's chair scraped against the kitchen linoleum. His face appeared in the doorway. "Let's get her to bed, Joan. I want her up and around tomorrow."

That night was a blur of pain, ice packs, and hands shaking Kiki every few hours to see if she was still alive. When daylight finally peeked around the window shade, she swam to aching consciousness at the piercing ring of a bell—the telephone.

At her father's groggy, "Hello?" Kiki drifted back to sleep. He spoke again, sounding more alert. "0700? Yes, sir. On the double."

The receiver clattered onto its hook. A door closed. There was the muffled sound of her parents talking.

****

"Girls, wake up! It's time to rise and shine!" Mrs. Moore leaned on her crutch in the bedroom doorway. For the first time since her fall she was dressed, wearing a starched cotton house-dress beneath one of Col. Moore's olive-drab wool jackets. A coffee mug steamed lazily in her free hand.

The springs on the top bunk creaked; Joan's flannel-covered legs dropped over the edge of the bed. "What's wrong, Mama? It's still dark outside."

"Your father was called to the base last night. I don't know when he's coming back—or if, " she said under her breath. "You'll have to help me get breakfast." Mrs. Moore paused. "Joan, can you light the pilot in the heater? It went out hours ago. Brr, it's cold!"

Kiki leaned out of the bottom bunk, wincing when she turned her shoulders. The coffee's fragrance filled the room. "I'm not going to school, am I, Mama?" Her whimper got only the shadow of a smile from her mother.

"We'll see. Try to get up. Don't bother getting dressed just yet."

After carefully getting out of bed, Kiki slipped into her old chenille bathrobe and shuffled to the kitchen. The glare from the bulb dangling over the kitchen table felt like needles piercing her eyes, and when she lowered herself into a chair, pain shot up her spine.

Joan came in, looking pert in saddle shoes, a white sweater, and a navy-blue pleated skirt. Her lily-of-the-valley toilet water upstaged the oatmeal's fragrance.

As she watched her sister through bloodshot eyes, Kiki wondered if she, herself, would live to be sixteen.

"I'll take over, Mama," Joan said. "You go sit down."

With a grateful smile, Mrs. Moore sunk into a chair. After Joan ladled the oatmeal into bowls, Kiki reached for the brown sugar. "Why did Daddy leave in the middle of the night? He's never done that before."

Mrs. Moore sighed. "Some emergency, most likely; I just

hope his unit hasn't been deployed."

The girls exchanged nervous glances. This was their mother's worst fear—that their father would be shipped out, going halfway around the world without them.

"Well, girls, there's nothing we can do about it, and we have work to do. Remember, no blabbing." Mrs. Moore took a spoonful of oatmeal.

Joan muttered, "Yeah, yeah. Loose lips sink ships."

Mrs. Moore looked up. "I'm in no mood for jokes. Those slogans are for good reason. Now, finish eating. Your ride will be here soon." She glanced at Kiki. "I think you can handle washing the breakfast dishes. Clear the table while I get the hot water going."

"So I'm staying home, Mama?" Kiki's voice was hopeful. "I'm still a little dizzy."

"Yes. I'll probably have to beg the school to let you go back, after your behavior yesterday." She gave Kiki a sour look.

As the morning crawled by, Kiki's headache subsided. It helped that her mother didn't stay mad, and that they were doing laundry. The spindly-legged washing machine, with its wringer suspended above the barrel-shaped tub, reminded Kiki of something out of <u>War of the Worlds</u>. Soapy water spurted out of a heavy black hose hooked over the sink edge, and the wringer clattered and groaned when wet laundry was fed through it. Under Mrs. Moore's supervision, the girls were sometimes allowed to work the ominous black rollers. The very real danger of losing a finger or two made this an exciting job.

When the washing was done, Kiki piled the wet clothes in the wicker basket and lugged them to the clothesline. Her mother hobbled along behind.

"These things will be stiff as boards in this cold air, but if the mist burns off, they'll dry." Mrs. Moore's teeth chattered as she balanced her crutch and wrestled laundry out of the basket, piece by piece.

Kiki inspected the clothespins before snapping them onto the wire. "No worms on 'em today."

"There probably never were any," Mrs. Moore's tone was flat.

Kiki's face reddened. "They were all over the clothespins and sheets—it was awful! Do you think we made it up?"

"That will be quite enough, Kiki!"

They finished in silence, Kiki clenching her jaw to keep from sassing back.

Mrs. Moore grasped her crutch to hobble back inside, turning to look at the clumsily hung laundry. "I guess this will have to do."

Kiki slouched into the kitchen and eased onto the seat of a hard-backed chair. She closed her eyes, thinking about the skull in the old house. If her mother thought they were lying about the maggots, what would she think of that?

Mrs. Moore sat down with a huff of relief, leaning her crutch against the wall and closing her eyes. At that moment the phone rang. Kiki jumped up to answer it.

"Moore residence, Kiki speaking."

"Get your mother to the phone, Kiki." It was Col. Moore. His voice had a tinny echo, like he was talking from a long distance.

"Daddy! We were worried about you."

"I need to talk to your mother. I don't have all day." His irritation came through the phone.

Kiki let the receiver dangle from the phone box and stepped back into the kitchen, grabbing the crutch. She slipped an arm under her mother's shoulder. "It's Daddy. He said you should hurry."

Mrs. Moore went to the phone. "Hi, Bill! Is everything okay?"

Kiki wandered into the room she and Joan shared, half-listening to the phone call. She ignored the pajamas piled on the floor, the unmade beds, and the homework folder sitting unopened on the chest of drawers. Snapping up the window's roller blind, she idly looked through the window. Across the way, in the old house, a shadow moved.

Mrs. Moore called, "Would you do an errand for me, Kiki? I want to make jam, and I'm almost out of paraffin; will you run to the Barrets' and get me some?"

Kiki, on the verge of saying, "I just saw something odd," saw her mother's face. There was a red spot on each cheek and her mouth was a straight, hard line.

"Yes'm. Uh, what's wrong, Mama? Is Daddy hurt?"

Mrs. Moore sagged against the doorway, putting a hand over her eyes. "Worse. He's being shipped out. He'll be home in a little while, but only to pack his duffel bag." She glared at Kiki. "You picked a fine time to run wild, with your father going off to war and me practically a cripple!"

She must have heard the panic in her own voice, or perhaps she saw the flush of guilt on Kiki's cheeks. At any rate, Mrs. Moore clasped her hands tightly, blinked several times, and said, "Now, please, go get that paraffin. I'll let Isabel Barret know you're coming." She stepped into the bathroom and snapped the door shut on a sob.

Chapter Twelve

Kiki started down the road, so full of worry she hardly saw the path ahead. Who would protect them from the ghost when Daddy left?

She ran for a while, finally slowing to a fast walk. Something made her look back; she was amazed to see Uncle Harry in the distance, bent forward and moving her way. She ducked off the path, hoping he hadn't noticed her, and watched from within the sprawling branches of a blackberry tangle. He was carrying something in one hand—it looked like a big gunnysack—and moving fast. His eyes were on the road, not the bushes. Kiki's first impulse was to run helter-skelter toward home—but, what if he caught her?

Some hard-shelled black bugs crawling on blades of grass near her hand caught her attention. Ticks? Eew! The sight of the blood-sucking insects spurred Kiki forward. She jerked off her red jacket, stuffed it under her less-colorful tan blouse, and crawled, elbows first, to the creek bed. From there it was just a stone's throw to the safety of the Barrets' rusted wire fence.

With a little slipping and sliding she got down, through and up the other side of the creek. When she crawled under the fence, stickers in her hair and shoes squishing mud, Pepper appeared, barking in an, "Oh, boy, a playmate!" sort of way. Beyond him, Mrs. Barret waved from her back steps.

"My goodness, Kiki, did you go through the creek? You're full of stickers, and wet, too. You'll catch your death of cold!"

Kiki smiled with relief. Mrs. Barret was probably the only person in the whole valley who wasn't mad at her. She asked for the paraffin, explaining that her mother was making jam.

"Why don't I drive you back home?" Mrs. Barret smiled. "I don't want you to get any colder and wetter than you already are."

Kiki's face brightened. A ride home—she'd be safe from

Uncle Harry! When she looked down at her shoes, though, she saw the sticky creek mud on the soles and the muddy speckles on her once-white anklets. Even her skirt was streaked with mud. Her smile faded. "I wouldn't want to get your car dirty."

"Just leave the shoes out here, child." Mrs. Barret's tone was brisk. "Come in and have some Ovaltine to take the chill off; we'll put papers down in the car." She gave Kiki a sharp look. "I want to hear all about your accident yesterday. Does your head still hurt? I hope you didn't get a concussion. You look a little peaked."

Kiki stepped out of her shoes. "I'm okay. Sorry about the mud. I had to hide from someone on the way here. Maybe I shouldn't come inside."

Mrs. Barret raised her eyebrows. "No, no, I won't hear of it. It wasn't a crime to be an adventurous child, last I heard!"

The kitchen was fragrant with the scents of cinnamon and apple. Kiki spotted two pies cooling beneath the stained-glass flowers of an ancient window. She pulled out a heavy, claw-footed chair to sit down, accepting the offer of a towel between her skirt and the seat cover.

"Can I cut you a piece of pie? I just took it out of the oven."

"Oh, yes, ma'am!"

As Mrs. Barret chattered, Kiki began to relax. It felt good, being clucked over like a wayward chick. She felt less afraid; safe.

Her neighbor pulled out another chair and sat down, saying, "Cat got your tongue? You're so quiet."

Kiki looked up quickly, wondering if Mrs. Barret could read minds.

"Did my mother tell you Daddy has to go overseas?" She paused. "Oh, no! I wasn't supposed to say anything—loose lips sink ships, you know."

"She did tell me, dear. It's just the details that we mustn't

90

spread around—and I don't know any of them. I don't imagine you do, either." Mrs. Barret smiled kindly. "I'm sure he wishes he could stay here, at least until your mother recuperates. But, with the war on, we don't always have a choice. Uncle Sam is relying on the men like your father, dear."

"Yes'm—that is, I know Daddy's been itching to get into the fight. He's even said so."

"Well, he needn't worry about his family while he's away. In this valley, everyone pitches in to help. With your mother laid up and your father overseas, you'll be well taken care of."

Kiki sighed. If only it was that easy.

They were quiet for a few minutes, Kiki eating pie and Mrs. Barret sipping tea.

When her fork scraped the plate's surface, Kiki said, "Mrs. Barret, why doesn't Uncle Harry tell Aunt Lou their daughter's not coming back?"

Mrs. Barret's cup clattered onto its saucer. "Oh, my! Well, dear, I don't know for sure. Maybe he's protecting her—she has a rather fragile grasp of reality." She glanced at the old Regulator clock on the wall. "Oh, look at the time! We'd better get you home." She hung her apron on a hook and slipped into a coat. "Just put your dish by the sink."

Kiki carried her plate to the drain-board. "What does that mean, 'fragile grasp on reality?'"

"It means she doesn't see things like the rest of us, dear." Mrs. Barret's voice was curiously flat. "You'd best leave that subject alone. It will only cause trouble."

Kiki looked away for a second. She didn't want to upset this new friend, but she just couldn't drop it.

"I think the ghost I've been seeing is their daughter. I think it's causing the bad stuff that's happening on our ranch." She swallowed, hard. "You believe me, don't you? You said there's a difference between dead and gone, where ghosts are concerned."

Mrs. Barret turned a serious face to Kiki. "Of the people who believe in ghosts—and that's not everyone, or even most everyone, you understand—some think the ghosts who remain where their bodies died are troubled spirits. Whether or not they cause problems is anybody's guess."

Kiki interrupted. "What do you mean, 'troubled'?"

"Well, dear, I'd say troubled could mean angry, upset, unhappy … just about any feeling that adds up to not being at peace. Yes, that's it."

"So," Kiki mused, "Rosalie June could still be here as a ghost, if she's a troubled spirit? But why would she be troubled? She had a nice home, even a boyfriend. Why would she run away, like people said she did? And, anyway, if she's a ghost now, she must have died. Doesn't anyone wonder what happened to her?"

Mrs. Barret looked surprised. "Wait a minute. Where did you get the idea she had a boyfriend? To my recollection she had a best girlfriend who spent a lot of time at the Partridge house—Brenda, her name was. I never saw Rosalie June with a boy, though." She looked thoughtful. "Brenda's folks were itinerant fruit pickers. They traveled the crop circuit. Brenda stayed with the Partridges a lot during the school year. She was a very sweet girl—even prettier than Rosalie June. The three of them, Brenda, Rosalie June and Lou, were always together. Harry was pretty much out of the loop back in those days."

They stepped out onto the porch, where Kiki put her shoes on. A few minutes later, settled in Mrs. Barret's car with her feet resting on a newspaper, Kiki said, "She did have a boyfriend. Maybe she had a best friend named Brenda, too; I don't know about that. Say, is Brenda still around? I mean, grown up, of course. Maybe we could find her."

"Absolutely not—you must know by now that Harry Partridge has no sense of humor where this subject is concerned. Why, he was in such a state when Rosalie June disappeared, he got in a fight with Brenda's father—her family left town because of it."

Mrs. Barret started the engine. "Let's go. Your mother's waiting for that paraffin."

They rode in silence a minute, Kiki praying her next words would come out right. "Mrs. Barret, there's a skeleton in the second story of the burnt house. I know, because I saw it." Her shoulders relaxed for the first time in days.

Isabel Barret jumped like a startled deer. The car stalled; she groaned, restarted it, and darted a sideways look at Kiki. "That's too far-fetched for even me to believe. If I've encouraged your wild imagination, I am sorry."

"But, it's true!" Kiki heard herself pleading.

"Not another word, now."

Kiki squeezed back tears and looked out the window. There was no sign of Uncle Harry. She wondered, staring at the bare winter orchard, what he'd been up to. Her mind flashed to the shadow she'd seen through her bedroom window.

****

"Come on in, Isabel. I'd love some company while I work on this jam." Kiki's mother took Mrs. Barret's coat and cleared a spot at the oilcloth-covered table.

In spite of the welcoming smile, Mrs. Moore's eyes were puffy. She looked pale, too—maybe because she wasn't wearing her usual red lipstick. Instead of sitting down, Isabel Barret tied an apron around her waist and walked over to the sink.

"You rest a minute, Emily, and let me finish this. I've been making jam since before you were born."

"Oh, my, what would I do without such lovely neighbors?" Mrs. Moore plopped down in the chair and burst into tears.

Kiki knelt next to her mother's chair, giving her a clumsy hug. "Don't cry, Mama. Everything's going to be all right. I'll be good from now on, I promise."

Mrs. Barret put an arm around her neighbor's shoulder.

"There, there now. Things must look very bleak, with Bill going overseas. This little ol' country ranch is probably the last place you want to be with two half-grown girls and a broken leg. But it will all work out. Remember what Mr. Churchill said, 'Things look darkest before the dawn.'"

Mrs. Moore lifted her head, wiping her eyes with the back of a hand. She gave her visitor a lopsided smile. "You're right, of course. Could you get me a hankie, Kiki?"

There was the thump of footsteps on the front porch. The door banged open and Col. Moore's voice called, "I'm home, Emily. I've got some stuff to bring inside."

Startled, Kiki looked from Mrs. Barret to her mother. "I'll go help." She grabbed her coat and ran out, aware that her headache was back.

Col. Moore acknowledged her presence with a nod. "Feeling better, I see. Guess you weren't hurt that bad." He reached into the truck. "Take this uniform, and don't let it drag in the mud." He scowled. "I haven't forgotten I owe you a whipping."

After pointing Kiki in the direction of a garment bag hanging over the back seat, he hefted an armload of boxes and climbed the front steps. Squeezing back tears, Kiki shouldered the heavy bag and went inside. When Mrs. Barret saw the girl struggling with the garment bag she lifted it off her shoulder, saying, "Where does this go, Emily?"

From the bedroom, Col. Moore called, "Good news, Emily. The C.O. gave us a couple extra days—his wife just had twins—so I'll have time to get things squared away around here." He came into the kitchen and put an arm around his wife, who was at the stove furiously stirring jam.

Kiki and Mrs. Barret went outside for another load of the colonel's things. A wisp of smoke drifted past the truck's front bumper.

Kiki frowned. "Where's that comin' from? Do you see that?"

Isabel Barret pulled open the car door. "What?"

"Right over there, see? It smells like wood smoke."

Mrs. Barret inhaled. "You're right. Is your mother burning trash?"

"No, ma'am. That's Joan's job, and she's not home. Maybe it's comin' from the Partridges' ranch."

"I don't think so. The wind isn't from that direction." Mrs. Barret walked slowly past the car, sniffing. "It's stronger over here, by the side of the house."

Kiki looked along the narrow space between the two buildings. Light flickered from one of the old house's windows.

"Look in there—what's that?"

Mrs. Barret gasped, "Oh, my goodness—flames! Run get your father!"

When Kiki followed her father out of the house a minute later, Mrs. Barret was already pulling the garden hose around from the back yard.

"Goddamn! There *is* smoke," Col. Moore shouted. "I thought she was lying again. Kiki, go turn on the spigot. I see it, Isabel," he continued. "I think it's comin' from inside."

Mrs. Barret handed him the hose, saying over her shoulder, "We saw flames in here!" She reached for the old brass doorknob.

"Stop!" Col. Moore's voice rang with authority. "Don't touch it. That metal may be hot enough to fry your skin— and we don't want smoke billowing out at us—Emily, call the Volunteer Fire Department!"

Col. Moore dragged the hose around the side of the building, barking commands as he moved. "Let's shoot some water in through one of the broken windows, and maybe on the wall next to our house. I'll be damned if I'll let the fire jump across and burn us out!"

Mrs. Moore came around the corner, picking her way along the uneven ground. "I called, Bill. Their truck was just down the road at the Grange Hall. They're on the way."

A siren's wail, getting louder by the second, sounded in the distance.

"I hear them!" Kiki exclaimed. She shivered, not knowing whether to be scared or excited. She'd never seen a house fire—Joan would be so jealous!

There was a small, "whoomp!" and light flashed from the window. Col. Moore, wielding the garden hose, waved to an ancient fire truck as it blundered up the gravel lane.

Kiki stood to one side, wondering if this was her chance to run away. Her eyes strayed to her mother's face; it was contorted with fear. With a sigh, she moved over, draping a skinny arm around Mrs. Moore.

"It's in there, boys." Col. Moore gestured with the water hose as the three firemen—Mr. Wendicott from the Grange Hall and his two teen-aged sons—scrambled to unwind a big canvas fire hose. Kiki grinned; Joan would miss this opportunity to flirt.

When a jet of water shot from the fire hose through one of the broken windows, smoke and steam billowed out. Within minutes the men were climbing up over the front threshold, Col. Moore in the lead. Then, from somewhere within, came an excited voice: "Over here, Pop. It's a doggone pile of burning rags!"

Someone coughed. Mr. Wendicott rasped, "I can't see a thing!"

More coughing, then, "Run get a shovel, Simon. Let's get these rags outside."

Shuffling, clomping sounds mingled with Mr. Wendicott's wheezing voice. "Homer, douse this floor." And, "Bill, you're gonna need to call the sheriff."

One of the Wendicott boys charged out the front door, running to the fire truck. Col. Moore hurried over to his wife.

"Go call the Sheriff, Emily. There's a pile of rags right in the middle of the room, and a powerful smell of kerosene. Someone torched it!"

Kiki's excitement turned to fear. Could a ghost start a fire? When the crew dumped the burning rags on open ground and began poking at them with the shovel, her fear gave way to curiosity. As she watched, the shovel exposed embroidery stitching, subdued against the sodden gray of the cloth around it. She moved closer for a better look. A faded green leaf and some letters, R – O – S   A – R – E, could be seen, worked in tiny, precise stitches. Kiki stared.

One of the young firemen turned to her. "Well, spit it out, kid. You know what that is; I can tell."

Kiki lifted her chin. "Who're you calling a kid, Skinny-bones?"

She took a moment to enjoy his embarrassed grin. "Our next-door neighbors have tea towels just like that."

Col. Moore, coming closer, looked down at the smoldering rags. "I do see some sewing on them. Could have belonged to anyone, though, and thrown in a rag bag long ago."

He turned to Kiki. "I'll mention it to the sheriff. But, if you're trying to get the Partridges in trouble, there'll be hell to pay."

Kiki blushed. The fireman, looking embarrassed, turned away.

Going up the front steps, Kiki heard Isabel Barret's quiet voice: "No, I believe she's right, Bill. I've seen towels like those hanging in Lou's kitchen many times."

The colonel's only response was a grunt.

Chapter Thirteen

It seemed like hours later that the firemen shook hands with Col. Moore, thanked Mrs. Moore for the coffee, and climbed back into the old fire truck. Kiki waved good-bye from the porch steps while balancing a tray of empty coffee cups on one arm, waitress style.

She turned her attention to Sheriff Hugh Madding, who was standing by the old house, clipboard in hand. She'd never seen a policeman before, up close—she figured a sheriff was really a country policeman. His rough green uniform reminded her of the men out at her father's army base, except that he wore a ranger hat and boots. He was taller than Col. Moore, but had the same sweaty smell and dark stubble on his weathered, serious face.

The colonel came around the corner, approached Sheriff Madding, and jerked a thumb toward Kiki. She didn't hear what he said, but the sheriff looked surprised. He stared at her, mouthing an emphatic, "Not on your life!"

Col. Moore rubbed his ash-covered chin, snapping, "Well, someone set this fire. Do you mean to tell me there's a firebug loose in the valley? Is my family in danger?"

Emily Moore's shocked face appeared on the other side of the screen door. She looked hard at Kiki, who mumbled, "I wouldn't ever play with fire, Mama. Doesn't Daddy know that?"

Mrs. Barret stepped outside. "It's time for me to get back home," she said. "It seems like days ago that we came up the road to deliver the paraffin."

At her car, she put one foot on the running board. "Emily, Lord knows you probably don't want to hear this, but I just have to speak up. You know as well as I do that this child had no opportunity to start that fire. First of all, she was at my house when she wasn't here with you this morning. Second, where in the world would she get kerosene, and how would she know to use it? And, while I'm on the subject, I might as well say I think it's time you took some of her ideas seriously!"

Mrs. Moore's face turned bright pink. Her temper was slow to ignite, but when it did, watch out. Half-turning away from Mrs. Barret, she said, "Well, I'm sure Kiki likes having you stand up for her, Isabel, even if it is her own mother you're taking to task; however, I do not appreciate it. You are absolutely right—she couldn't have started the fire. But her other behavior, and the way she's been prying into the Partridges' lives, well, she needs a spanking for all of that. She doesn't need you undermining our discipline."

Mrs. Barret looked as if she'd been slapped. She snapped her mouth shut and jammed her pocketbook under her arm. Kiki leaned forward, tugging at her mother's sleeve.

"Er, Mama?" After one look at her mother's face, Kiki turned away. She wondered if she'd ever be allowed to talk to Mrs. Barret again.

Through clenched teeth, Mrs. Moore said, "Before you leave, Isabel, what are these, 'ideas,' I should take so seriously?"

Kiki held her breath. Was Mrs. Barret going to mention the ghost?

Col. Moore, walking over to the women, growled an interruption. "Emily, you've been out here in the cold long enough. If you're done giving your statement to the sheriff, go back inside."

He turned to Mrs. Barret. "Thanks for your help during this fiasco, Isabel. I imagine you've got chores to do, back at your own place." His tone was firm, dismissing. He took his wife by the arm and led her up the front steps.

Mrs. Barret, her face showing more hurt than anger, got into her car and slammed the door shut. Kiki's stomach tightened—people were mad at each other, and it was her fault. One grubby fist wiped away a tear. Someone had tried to help her, and look what happened.

Sheriff Madding approached Mrs. Barret's car as it rolled across the gravel. She stopped, cranking her window down. He leaned in as far as his hat would go, pointing to something on his clipboard. She nodded. He straightened up, tapped her car in a *get going* signal, and walked back to the house.

The colonel answered his knock. "Got everything you need, Sheriff? I signed off on all your forms, I think." He started to shut the door.

"Hold on a second, Col. Moore." The sheriff set his clipboard on the porch railing and looked down at Kiki hovering in the shadow of the porch. "Are you the younger daughter? Your neighbor mentioned you."

Col. Moore looked through the screen door. "What're you doing still out there, Kiki? Get inside!" He started unbuckling his belt, and she knew there was no way to get through the door without getting at least one vicious swat. She took an unwilling step forward.

"Hold on a minute, Colonel. I have to talk to you and this girl. Step back outside, please." Sheriff Madding's voice was soft, but his words were clipped, like he was mad about something.

Col. Moore's face got red. "I already told you, Sheriff. With orders to ship out in a matter of hours, I have a lot to do and not much time to do it. If you don't mind, I'm fed up with talking about that damned fire."

Kiki stopped, wondering why the sheriff wanted to talk to her. Did he know she'd skipped school? She avoided her father's stare and looked at Sheriff Madding. "I wasn't here when the fire started, sir." She was surprised how calm she sounded—she felt like throwing up.

The sheriff pushed his hat back and sat down on the top step, giving Kiki a friendly nod. "Sit down a minute, kid."

After glancing at her father, Kiki perched on the bottom step. Col. Moore leaned one shoulder against the door frame, grumbling, "Okay. Let's get this over with. What do you need, Sheriff?"

Sheriff Madding looked down at Kiki. "I heard you were upstairs in that building yesterday. Is that true?"

Kiki gulped, swallowed wrong, managed to choke out, "Yes, sir. I fell off the stairwell and got hurt—my head, mostly."

The sheriff spoke very quietly. "I understand you found something … surprising up there."

Kiki threw a frightened look at her father, now squatting on his haunches and looking interested. He spoke. "Is that right, Kiki? You found something up there? What?"

She couldn't look at him. With both of the men so close, Kiki felt corralled. She squeezed her eyes shut. "I found a pile of furniture that looked like an island," she whispered, "I mean, there were some old chairs around a mattress—kind of like guards—and rope tied like a fence. The mattress was falling apart. There were rats, too." She shivered. Panic engulfed her as she saw herself, once again, in the gloomy attic. She covered her mouth, suddenly nauseous.

The sheriff put a meaty hand on her shoulder. "Just take your time, girl. What else did you see?"

She said, through her fingers, "I saw bones and a skull in the middle of the mattress. The skull had eye holes and gray teeth." She pulled her knees up to her chin, hiding her face. "I didn't mean to bother it. I just wanted to get the sheet for my mother. I didn't know anything was up there. I promise I won't tell anyone."

Col. Moore sat open-mouthed, staring at Kiki. He shook his head. "Are you making this up?" He looked at the sheriff. "She's got the damnedest imagination. First, she thinks those burned rags came from the Partridges—now she's seeing skeletons. What's next?"

Both men got to their feet, towering above Kiki. The sheriff said, "Is this the truth, girl? It's hard to believe. You sure you didn't make it up?"

She scrambled off the step. "I'll swear on a stack of bibles."

Sheriff Madding passed a hand across his eyes. "That won't be necessary." Then, "I need to use your phone, Col. Moore—this is gonna take a while." As he went into the house he called back over his shoulder, "We'll probably have to go in through that upstairs window."

Kiki's father slammed a fist down on the porch railing. "Christ on a crutch! What next? I'm beginning to wish we'd never bought this god-forsaken place!"

Just then a truck chugged up the road, its engine roar competing with music and laughter from the cab. It was Joan's ride home from school. The driver made a reckless turn, sprayed gravel, and stopped by the porch. Joan climbed down, waving a cheerful goodbye. She stopped at the porch. "What's going on? What stinks? Is that a police car?" She glanced around, fluffing her hair. "Are you in trouble again, Kiki? What did I miss?"

Mrs. Moore came to the door, gave Joan a smile-erasing look, and said, "Come inside, girls." She leaned heavily on her crutch, biting off each word. "There was a fire, Joan. Someone tried to burn down the old house. The sheriff is here, and more police are coming."

Joan's mouth made a big O. "A fire? Oh, my gosh! Was anyone hurt?"

Mrs. Moore shook her head. "No. Now, inside, on the double!"

A few minutes later, in the girls' bedroom, Joan threw down her books and began changing from her school clothes. She slipped an old sweater over her head, reached through one armhole, and patted the top of Kiki's head. "You got the look of a person who thinks everything's her fault. Is it?"

Kiki threw herself on the bottom bunk. Her sister leaned over, murmuring, "Or, is that what they think—Mama and Daddy? Well, don't worry. I'll stick up for you." She gave Kiki a quick smile and sauntered out of the bedroom, moaning, "I'm starving. Are there any of those cookies left?"

Through the bedroom window, Kiki watched her father put the ladder against the smoke-blackened wall next door. She rubbed her head and slouched into the kitchen, wondering how the ghost was reacting to these intrusions.

From her spot at the table, Joan raised plucked eyebrows. "What?"

Kiki went to the sink. "I'll finish washing the dishes—Mama's busy packing Daddy's duffel bag." She picked up the dishrag to rub absentmindedly at a plate. "It's not just the fire, Joan. I had to tell that sheriff what I saw up in the old house. Now Daddy's afraid he'll miss out on going overseas with his unit—all because of me."

She turned an agonized face to Joan. "Will you stick up for me about that? Huh, Joan?"

Joan popped a graham cracker in her mouth, wiped her lips on the back of her hand, and said, "What'd you see? Oh, never mind. I probably wouldn't believe it, anyway." She walked out of the kitchen. "Mama, could you use some help?"

Kiki stared down at the soaking crockery. Salty tears ran into the dishwater.

Some ally, she thought. She began on the dishes—rub with the rag, dip plate in rinse water, set plate in drainer. Pick up another plate, repeat process. With a sigh, she switched to thoughts of her newest Wonder Woman comic book. The sound of a siren, barely discernible at first, screamed up the lane.

Car doors slammed. Men's voices, excited, called, "Whatcha got, Sheriff?"

"Somebody murdered?"

"Coroner's on his way."

Kiki dropped the dishrag into the sink. She turned to see Joan coming out of their parents' room, stage-whispering, "Did you really find a body in the old house? Cuz if you're making it up, they'll find out, now. I sure wouldn't wanta be you if you're lying."

Kiki hoped her face didn't show her panic. She stuck her tongue out at Joan, who laughed and said, "Let's watch from our room."

Chapter Fourteen

From beyond the bedroom window the ladder was in full view, stacked full of men: Sheriff Madding at the top, another man—a deputy, Kiki figured, since he was in a uniform—in the middle, and her father at the bottom. A deputy stood on the ground, steadying the ladder.

The sheriff's voice was clear: "We're gonna have to take out this windowpane. Can't be helped, Colonel."

Col. Moore nodded. The deputy on the ground handed up a hammer, Sheriff Madding swung it, and CRACK! The glass shattered.

Kiki's bedroom window creaked and slid up. The fragrance of roses floated in. Something brushed against her shoulder, sending a shiver up her spine. She turned around, expecting to see Joan, and gasped at the sight of Rosalie June, close enough to touch.

The ghost nodded to her, eyes bright. A whispery sound came from her mouth. "I want my mother."

Then, before Kiki had time to blink, the ghost was gone. Every hair on Kiki's body stood at attention. Her legs buckled; she sat down on the floor, hard. "Joan!" she yelled, shrill and scared.

Her sister stepped into the room, looking at Kiki on the floor. "What're you doing down there? If you're hiding from those deputies, don't bother. They're not interested in tomboys." She wrapped a strand of hair around her finger.

Kiki groaned. "I don't feel so good." She stood up to leave the room—she'd had all she could take of Joan and the scene beyond the window. Her sister nodded vacantly, ogling the men on the ladder.

In their parents' bedroom, Emily Moore hobbled back and forth from the closet to the half-stuffed duffel bag, packing her husband's clothes. She looked like she'd lost her best friend.

Kiki cleared her throat. "Why don't you sit down, Mama? I can do this. Just tell me what to put in the bag."

"I'm almost finished." Mrs. Moore pushed her hair back from her face, avoiding her daughter's eyes.

Kiki crossed the room in two steps, wrapping an arm around her mother's waist. "Please don't worry. Everything's going to be okay." She paused. "I'm really sorry I've caused you so much trouble." She stared at the floor.

"Why, Kiki," Mrs. Moore said, sounding surprised. Apologies didn't happen much in this household. She leaned her face against Kiki's cheek. "It's not a perfect world, honey."

Kiki had an inspiration. "Let's call Mrs. Barret and ask her to come back. I know she didn't want to fight with you. She was just worried about me—and you, too; our whole family, I bet."

Mrs. Moore was quiet for a minute, twisting one of Daddy's undershirts in her hands. "You could be right. She certainly took a risk, saying what she did." She looked out the window. "But the sheriff won't want extra people around while he's dealing with that—that thing up there."

Joan piped up from the doorway, "Hey, look. They're getting ready to take something out of the house—they're hauling up a stretcher! I'm just itching to call my friends. Imagine, a real live skeleton on our property—no one at school can top this!"

Mrs. Moore looked horrified. "My goodness, Joan, you certainly can *not* call your friends. Do you think this is a side show attraction?" She sat down on the bed. Her shoulders sagged. "You're right, Kiki. Isabel knew better than I did. She knew you were telling the truth. I'll call her right now."

Joan ran to the phone. "Let me call her, Mama. Please? I've just got to tell someone, and I know she'll listen to me!"

Mrs. Barret arrived within minutes of Joan's excited call, an apron peeking out from under her coat. Kiki led her to the kitchen table, where Mrs. Moore sat, looking sheepish.

"Thank you for coming, Isabel. I wouldn't have blamed you if you hadn't, after what I said. I'm so sorry."

Mrs. Barret pulled a chair away from the table and sat down. "Don't give it another thought, Emily. I probably overstepped my bounds, speaking as I did. I'm sorry, too." She cocked her head toward the noise outside. "What's all that?"

Joan piped up, "They're exploring the attic. They're finding all sorts of creepy things—isn't it exciting?"

Mrs. Moore's look silenced Joan. "Get us some coffee."

Mrs. Barret sighed. "So much trouble for your family, Emily; you must be wondering what you got into, buying this ranch."

Mama's smile wavered. She glanced at her daughters. "Get to your chores, girls. I want to talk with Isabel alone."

"I'm waiting for the coffee to perk," Joan said.

Both girls dawdled by the stove until their mother glared at them, saying, "And, Joan, I don't want to hear you on the telephone gossiping about this."

Joan scowled as she poured coffee from the speckled enamel pot, sloshing it over onto the saucers. She threw her sister an evil look.

Mrs. Barret said, "The fire's out—why is everyone still here?"

"Well, from what I understand," Mrs. Moore's voice sounded cautious. "There might be something terrible in the attic. Kiki says she saw *a skeleton*. Can you imagine?"

Mrs. Barret blew on the scalding coffee, took a sip, said nothing.

"I didn't believe it, at first." Mrs. Moore continued. "But the sheriff thinks it's worth investigating. He said that could be why someone started the fire." She paused. "Looks like Kiki was telling the truth, this time."

Joan, looking ready to burst, moved closer to the table. "Someone was trying to cover up a murder!"

Mrs. Moore gave a small shriek. "For heaven's sake, don't

even think such a thing. We have to live here—and without your father, soon!"

"If there is a body, the person probably died a long time ago." Mrs. Barret looked thoughtful.

"Well, then, maybe it was a tramp—I bet he climbed up there when the ranch was vacant." Joan giggled, sounding nervous.

Kiki cleared her throat. "The bones looked really old—and the cloth was rotten, like it's been there a long time. But, how could anyone get to the second floor with the staircase gone?"

Joan snorted. "You did, didn't you?"

"We shouldn't be making idle guesses," their mother said. "I think we can agree Kiki was trying to help, and things would be much simpler if she hadn't. What she stumbled onto is in the sheriff's hands now. You're not in trouble any more, Kiki."

Everyone at the table looked relieved. Kiki grinned, planting a kiss on her mother's cheek just as someone knocked at the front door.

Mrs. Moore looked at Kiki. "Get that, will you, honey?"

Kiki opened the door, expecting to see a deputy; instead, Uncle Harry's watery eyes glowered at her. She gripped the doorknob, staring dumbly at him. With a curt nod, he pushed past her and into the room.

When he saw Mrs. Moore, Uncle Harry growled, "Emily, what's going on out there? Those snot-nosed Boy Scouts tried to run me off the property." His rumbling voice rose. "Lou and I have been living in this valley a lot of years. We deserve to know what you people are up to!"

Kiki slipped behind him into the kitchen. Her mother and Mrs. Barret both looked startled, and a little scared.

Harry continued, more quietly, "What in tarnation are they looking for up in that old rattrap? Far as I know, it doesn't even have a decent floor, much less anything else.

110

What made the sheriff think he should go nosing around? The place has burned before; it'll probably burn again. It's not like someone died."

Kiki's mother stood, using the back of her chair for support. "As a matter of fact, Harry, they think someone did die in there, a long time ago."

Mrs. Barret nodded. "No one's lived in that house for years, have they, Harry? Not since what's his name—Herschfeldt—ran off after the first fire."

"Yes, Herschfeldt; his name was Herschfeldt, may he rot in hell!" Harry turned to glare at Kiki. "I suppose you've got everyone believing you've seen a ghost, too!" He pushed past her and strode out the front door.

Joan jumped up, bursting with excitement. "Mama, he's going out there! Can we go, too?"

Mrs. Moore looked resigned. "All right. I had no idea Harry was so difficult. Stay out of his way, girls."

As they rounded the corner of the house, the girls saw Uncle Harry arguing with the deputy at the bottom of the ladder—a kid who looked like a high school police cadet.

They were in time to hear, "Uh, sir? Sheriff Madding don't want nobody hanging around 'til we get done with the …." He paused, maybe searching his mind for some polite word, "… the remains."

Kiki could tell this deputy wasn't used to giving orders; sweat trickled across his pimply forehead.

"I ain't Nobody, boy! What in the hell's going on?"

The deputy clamped his mouth shut. His Adam's apple wobbled. Kiki tried not to smile.

Uncle Harry continued, "How old are you, anyway? Don't I know your parents?"

At that moment, Sheriff Madding stuck his head out the window. "Robert, I told you to keep the area clear. And hand me up the Brownie. We're going to need photos of this scene."

He looked down at Uncle Harry, who now had one foot

on the ladder. In a quieter voice, the sheriff said, "This is a crime scene, sir. I'll have to ask you to leave." He waited while Harry, looking like a thunderstorm about to happen, stepped back. With a glance at Robert, who was now returning from the truck with the camera, Sheriff Madding moved back into the depths of the building.

Mrs. Moore, leaning on her crutch, swung around the corner. "We have to do what the sheriff says, Harry. If there's really a dead body in there, none of us needs to see it. I certainly don't need the nightmares—neither do my girls." Her voice was firm. She put a hand on Harry's arm and smiled sweetly up at him. "Do you want me to have Bill call you when they're done? He'll likely appreciate your help sorting this out before he has to leave."

Harry looked embarrassed. He shuffled his feet, muttered something, and let Mrs. Moore lead him around to the front of the house. Kiki and Joan trailed behind them, fascinated at their mother's cleverness. They watched Harry stomp away through the orchard.

"All right, the show's over," Mrs. Moore said. "Get back inside where you belong." To Mrs. Barret, standing nearby, she said, "You'd think that skeleton was his long lost brother or something!"

Joan chimed in, "What a grouch! How can Aunt Lou stand him?"

Kiki realized it was time to speak up. "Do you think that man, Herschfeldt, killed someone and left them up there?" She wanted to say, 'like Rosalie June?'

Mrs. Moore rolled her eyes. "That's enough, Kiki. This isn't one of your <u>Nancy</u> <u>Drew</u> mysteries."

"But, Mama!" Kiki looked to Mrs. Barret, hoping for an ally. Isabel Barret had her face turned and was staring vacantly out across the orchard.

"Let's go, girls," their mother snapped. "Joan, the chickens are beginning to make a ruckus—they want their feed." She looked at Kiki. "Go in and peel some potatoes. I don't know when we'll be eating, but let's get something started."

Mrs. Moore hobbled back into the house, Kiki and Mrs. Barret trailing along behind. Joan moved off toward the hen house. The back door had barely closed when Joan squealed, "What're you bringing out? Oh, my gosh!"

"I'll handle this, Emily." Mrs. Barret stepped to the doorway. "Joan! Your mother wants you to get to those chickens, and then come inside."

Joan flounced in a few minutes later, her face one huge pout. "Why can't we watch? We're missing everything, Mama!"

Kiki, intent on fading into the background so she could slip outside, made the mistake of catching her sister's eye. An evil grin spread across Joan's face.

"Say, Kiki, do you think the ghost you saw in that attic could have been from the skeleton?"

Mrs. Moore closed her eyes, frowning. She looked tired. "All right, Joan, what kind of trouble are you trying to start? You know we don't talk such nonsense."

Both girls slouched against the kitchen sink. Kiki gulped. "It's true, Mama. I saw the ghost of a girl—the girl in the picture on Aunt Lou's window sill."

Outside, Sheriff Madding shouted, "Easy does it! That's it, tilt it just a bit more—careful, will you, this thing is damn fragile! Col. Moore, are you bringing up the rear?"

Joan grabbed Kiki's hand and dragged her from the kitchen. "The bedroom window—we can see from there!"

As they watched, the girls saw two deputies step out of the old house's second-story window and back nervously down the ladder. The stretcher suspended between them looked empty except for a canvas draped over it.

"Must not be much of a skeleton," was Joan's comment. "Maybe it was a child." She looked at Kiki. "I don't like this. I'm getting scared."

Well, finally, Kiki thought.

Chapter Fifteen

When the stretcher reached the ground, Sheriff Madding directed the deputies to a covered truck out front. His face was grim.

The youngest deputy, the one who had run up against Uncle Harry, held the back of the stretcher. He suddenly twisted to one side, shuddering.

"Is he gonna drop it? What's bothering him?" Joan sounded fascinated.

The air around the youth flickered. In a blend of light and shadow, Kiki saw Rosalie June clinging to the stretcher. The ghost's hand opened—something fell to the ground.

"Hold it steady, Robert. What's got into you?"

Another deputy chuckled, saying, "Maybe someone just walked over Robert's grave." Robert blushed, scowling.

When the stretcher and its burden were maneuvered into the back of the truck, the vehicle pulled away down the lane. The deputies walked back to the old house, talking quietly. At the ladder, Robert saw the girls watching. He pushed back his shoulders and gave them a small salute. Joan, a dreamy smile on her lips, murmured, "I just love a man in a uniform, don't you?"

Kiki tried not to gag.

Col. Moore came down the ladder and moved out of sight.

"Let's go!" Joan said.

The girls raced through the kitchen and down the back steps, sliding to a sudden stop at the sight of their parents and Mrs. Barret.

"Well, it's gone," Col. Moore said. "Madding said they'll be a while up there—told me to go on about my business. Thank God for small favors." He looked worn out. "Is Harry still here? The sheriff wants a word with him."

Mrs. Barret frowned. "He left a few minutes ago, Bill."

Col. Moore jerked a thumb at Kiki. "Run after him. Those guys won't clear out of here until Madding gets his paperwork done."

"Yes, sir." Kiki moved slowly to the front yard, hoping Harry was gone. When she passed the ladder her foot caught on a rung and down she went, hands first into the stubbly grass. Something hard dug into her palm—a ragged cloth pouch lay in the weeds. The finger she stuck inside it touched metal, and she pulled out a tarnished cross.

Kiki tucked the cross into her pocket and dawdled toward the orchard. No sign of Uncle Harry—she counted to sixty and turned back.

****

"He must've walked really fast, Daddy. I didn't see him, honest."

"Dammit, girl, can't you do anything right?"

Kiki stared at the ground, thinking, No, I guess I can't.

Sheriff Madding came up behind them. "It's probably just as well, Colonel. I need to talk to both of the Partridges." He looked around the yard. "We're not finished here, but we'll wrap things up for today."

To Kiki, he said, "Don't go in that building, do you hear? That's a police order." He gave her an apologetic smile.

The ladies both got a tip of his hat as the sheriff prepared to leave. "I appreciate your cooperation. We'll be back tomorrow to finish up, and then we'll be out of your hair for good."

"Colonel." The sheriff crossed the ground to stand before Col. Moore. "You'd best let your C.O. know you'll be needed here until everything's wrapped up." He nodded to the deputies. "Okay boys, let's go."

When the trucks left, Col. Moore let out a string of curses. "That dime-store cop actually thinks he can tell the Army what to do!"

An hour later, Kiki puttered at the sink while Joan struggled with algebra equations at the kitchen table. It was supper-time, but their parents were still in the bedroom with the door closed. They had been in there, voices quiet but intense, for what seemed like ages.

Joan put down her pencil. "Are they figuring out where we should live while Daddy's overseas? I mean, he won't make us stay here, will he, since they found that body?"

Kiki looked at her sister, surprised. Was Joan scared? Weren't high school kids supposed to be tough? "Well, I doubt we'd go live with the grandparents in Minnesota—Mama always says she never looked back when she and Daddy ran off to get married. So where does that leave us?"

The phone rang. Before either of the girls could get it, Col. Moore was out of the bedroom and lifting the receiver. He spoke quietly, finishing with, "We'll be over shortly. Thank you." He leaned into the kitchen. "Girls, we've been invited to supper by Mrs. Partridge. Go get cleaned up."

"Did the sheriff talk to them?" Kiki brightened, thinking maybe Uncle Harry wasn't mad at her anymore.

Col. Moore growled, "Damned if I know. Finish up there."

Within minutes Joan and Kiki were waiting at the front door, hair brushed and faces washed.

"I don't want to go." Kiki murmured.

Joan's lip curled. "Don't be an idiot. They invited us, didn't they? Just behave yourself, and everything will be okay. Maybe they'll offer to let us stay with them while Daddy's overseas."

Kiki raised an eyebrow, ready to ask Joan what alternate universe she lived in, when their father's voice called, "Get in the back of the truck, you two. Your mother and I will be right out."

The girls climbed into the back of the truck and sat across from each other on the wheel wells. Joan, skirt folded primly around her legs, looked very ladylike. Kiki tried to cover her knobby knees with the hem of her skirt, but it was hopeless.

She gave Joan a forlorn look; would she ever be pretty like her sister?

Col. Moore came back outside, carrying his wife in his arms. The air filled with their laughter and her lilac sachet. When she was settled in the cab he jumped in, revved the engine, and yelled, "Hold on back there!"

They bumped down the road, mud spewing from the tires.

****

Aunt Lou greeted them at the back gate. "Come on in. Dinner's ready. Harry'll be in as soon as he's finished the chores."

When she escorted them into the front parlor, Kiki hung back, hoping to sneak away. Her father gripped her arm and whispered, "Oh, no, you don't. You're not pulling any tricks tonight."

Stale air and furniture polish permeated the room. The upright piano, its lid shut, hovered silently between a stodgy plush sofa and a spindly-legged armchair. Kiki walked over, lifted the piano lid, and touched the keys. At the sound of the first note, pages of sheet music wavered and fell from the music rack. Kiki picked them up and put them back, looking around nervously.

Across the room on the pantry pass-through, sparkling glass tumblers, embroidered napkins, and cheese-stuffed celery sticks caught her attention. She lifted a napkin and read: "Roses are red, violets are blue, sugar is sweet and so are you."

"Help yourself, dear." Aunt Lou's plump arm reached for the tray of snacks. "Have one and pass these, will you?"

Kiki dropped the napkin and attempted a casual smile.

Aunt Lou continued, "I was so surprised when Harry suggested we have your family over tonight. He's not usually so neighborly—standoffish, I call him." She smiled at Mrs. Moore. "Your girls will be a comfort to you while Bill is gone, Emily. You just don't know how lucky you are to have them."

118

Mrs. Moore's smile disappeared. Her husband cleared his throat. "Say, Lou, did the sheriff get hold of you? He wanted to talk to you and Harry. I'm not sure why—probably needs your help, since you know everyone around here."

They all looked at Aunt Lou. She squeezed her hands together. "Well, he might have talked with Harry; I really don't know. I was in town." She looked thoughtful. "When I got home, Harry was in an awful mood. He did cheer up enough to have me invite you for supper."

The phone rang, two longs and two shorts—the party-line ring for the Moores' house. Aunt Lou looked at Joan. "Answer that please, dear."

"Yes, Ma'am." Joan went to the phone on the kitchen wall. "Hello?" She listened for a second, then stage-whispered, "It's for you, Daddy—the sheriff."

Aunt Lou's face flushed. "We shouldn't have answered it."

Mrs. Moore leaned back to look up at Aunt Lou standing above her. Kiki shivered, because, at that moment, Aunt Lou looked like a soft, pink-and-white-turkey vulture.

Kiki sidled toward the parlor doorway, hoping to overhear her father's conversation. She glanced at Joan's calm, almost angelic face—her sister was up to something.

A moment later Joan asked, "Did you see the fire, Aunt Lou? It was out by the time I got home from school." She pushed out her lower lip in a very good imitation of a whimper. "And I didn't get to see the body, either. I wonder who it was?"

Mrs. Moore's eyes narrowed. "You should be glad you missed all that, Joan. It was awful." She paused. "This couldn't have happened at a worse time, with me hurt and Bill…." Her voice trailed off.

A clock ticked somewhere close by. Out in the kitchen, Col. Moore's voice rumbled on.

Aunt Lou cleared her throat. "I saw the smoke, of course, and heard the sirens. The rest of it—you must be mistaken!"

She looked around to each of them. "Let's not talk about that, now. I want this evening to be fun."

Col. Moore finished the phone call and returned to the table. "Sheriff's comin' out, Lou. It'll disrupt your dinner, but I couldn't talk him out of it." He turned to Kiki. "Run out and tell Harry."

Kiki gave her sister a pleading look. For once Joan got the unspoken message—she turned, saying smoothly, "Oh, please, let me go, too, Daddy. You know how pokey she is. You probably want to see Uncle Harry sometime before next year."

The colonel nodded his approval and the girls hurried outside. As they approached the barn, Joan bumped Kiki's shoulder. "You owe me one, kid. It wasn't easy to leave those yummy snacks."

"Thanks, Joan. I don't think I could face Uncle Harry by myself, no matter what he told Daddy." She stopped in front of the barn's big double doors. They were closed and locked. "He's not in there. Wonder where he is?"

Joan walked around to where Harry's truck was usually parked, saying, "Looks like he drove somewhere. Let's go tell them."

Kiki paused. "We should at least yell for him, just in case. Aunt Lou said he was out here."

Joan nodded, cupping her hands to her mouth. "Uncle Harry! Uncle Harry!"

The only response was the surprised crowing of a rooster. Kiki went to the barn door, put her mouth up to the crack between the two sides, and shouted, "Uncle Harry!"

There was a muffled, "Woof."

The girls jumped back, startled. Joan said, "Wherever he went, he didn't take Sparky along. The poor thing's locked in there."

They ran back to the kitchen, Joan in the lead and full of importance. "We couldn't find him, Daddy. And you know what? The truck's not there."

Aunt Lou, lifting a savory roast out of the oven, straightened and gave the girls an irritated glance. "Well, for goodness sake, where is that man? He knows supper's at six. It's not like him to go off without telling me—and with company here!"

Mrs. Moore said, "Why don't you go ahead and put the food on the table, Lou? Maybe we can finish before the sheriff gets here. When Harry comes in, we'll explain why we started without him."

Aunt Lou sighed. "You're right. We should eat. Roast beef has to be eaten as soon as it's ready—Harry knows that."

Mrs. Moore turned to Joan and Kiki. "Go wash your hands, girls."

Kiki watched as the colonel helped Mama to the dining room table. She felt an unusual bit of sympathy for him—all this bad stuff happening just as he finally had a chance to go off to war.

She was spooning out a second helping of candied carrots when the crunch of tires on gravel sounded outside.

Col. Moore pushed his chair back. "Harry or the sheriff, one or the other," he said.

"That didn't sound like Harry's truck." Aunt Lou stood, moving quickly to look out the kitchen window.

A knock rattled the screen door. The sheriff's voice said, "We sure hate to disturb you at dinnertime, ma'am."

Col. Moore, raising his eyebrows at his wife, left the table to join Aunt Lou. Mrs. Moore got her crutch, said to the girls, "Stay here and finish your dinner," and followed him.

Kiki and Joan scraped the last morsels of food from their plates while keeping an eye on the adults in the kitchen. "Listen, but pretend to eat," Joan whispered.

Sheriff Madding and two deputies—but not the young, cute one—stood just inside the back door. The sheriff glanced into the dining room at the food-laden table. "We'll try to make this short, so you can get back to your meal." His gaze stopped at Uncle Harry's empty plate. "Where's Mr. Partridge?

Isn't he here?"

Aunt Lou snapped, "He's a little late getting in from chores. He'll be along soon. What on earth would he know about that fire, anyway?"

The girls looked at each other. Joan slipped out of her chair to hover in the doorway, whispering, "Something's fishy."

Chapter Sixteen

Kiki eased off her chair and went to stand behind Joan. From around her sister's shoulder she saw Sheriff Madding rubbing his chin, his face grave.

"Well, ma'am, you weren't at the Moores' ranch earlier today; maybe you aren't aware of everything." He glanced at the two girls listening in the doorway and cleared his throat. "I got my staff busy reading our files for the last 30-40 years—that's how old we estimate those, er, remains, to be."

The two deputies squirmed, looking longingly at the food on the table.

Sheriff Madding leaned in toward Aunt Lou. "Your daughter disappeared just about that long ago, didn't she, Mrs. Partridge? According to our records, she was never found."

"What has that got to do with anything, Sheriff?" Aunt Lou's voice was high-pitched, strained.

With a quick glance at Col. and Mrs. Moore, the sheriff said, "Let's find Partridge before we go any further." He turned to the deputies. "We'll round him up while these folks finish their supper."

A flush crept up Col. Moore's neck. He folded his arms in what Kiki thought of as his 'commanding-officer' pose. "Now hold on, Sheriff. We can eat later. Get on with your questions. You don't need Partridge; you already talked to him."

Madding rocked back on his heels. "I wish I could accommodate you, Colonel." He glanced at Aunt Lou. "Where did you say your husband is—doing chores? Where's his truck?"

Aunt Lou gave an exasperated sigh. She stared at the floor.

Col. Moore looked confused. "Does he use his truck for chores, Lou?"

Aunt Lou opened her mouth, snapped it shut, opened it again. "Not usually. Why does it matter? What has this to do with the fire—or what you say you found in the old house?"

She scowled at the sheriff. "I don't believe there's anything in that attic—certainly not a dead body; who on earth would leave a body in that wreck of a house? I've never heard such nonsense in all my life!"

The sheriff ran a finger around the inside of his shirt collar.

"I agree with you ma'am, up to a point. There hasn't been much worth noting in this valley, years on end." He shook his head almost imperceptibly at the deputy edging toward the basket of rolls. "There was that one incident, though—the disappearance of your daughter. The skeleton we found may close that case."

The color drained from Aunt Lou's face. She gripped the back of a chair, knuckles showing white. "My daughter? Rosalie June? How dare you imply such a terrible thing!" She turned to Mama, fear gleaming in her eyes. "Emily, can you make any sense of this? My girl's not dead. She ran away. Ask Harry!"

Mama stepped over to slip an arm around Aunt Lou's shoulders. "Let's just sit down for a minute. When Harry comes in, he'll explain everything." She gave Sheriff Madding a withering look.

Aunt Lou perched on the edge of a kitchen chair, staring at the spotless linoleum floor. Her head jerked up. "What about the other fire—the one that happened years ago, when Rosalie June ran away? And Herschfeldt, the man who lived there—he disappeared, and good riddance. Maybe it was his remains up there. Where's that report?"

Madding studied his fingernails. "That file was closed, Mrs. Partridge. Seems Herschfeldt just left—couldn't make a go of ranching, or he moved on for some other reason—it wasn't a man's body we found."

Daddy cleared his throat. "It seems to me, Sheriff, you should be concentrating on making my ranch safe from firebugs, not trying to figure out answers to something that happened a helluva long time ago."

Sheriff Madding got to his feet. "We're working on it, Colonel. Right now we need to find Mr. Partridge. Let's go, boys." He jerked his chin toward the door.

Kiki squared her shoulders and leaned around Joan. "Sheriff, did you figure out where those rags came from—the ones that started the fire? 'Cause there's some just like 'em in there." She pointed at the napkins lying on the pass-through.

Aunt Lou jumped to her feet. "What on earth? Are you making trouble for us, you hateful girl?"

Kiki flinched. When Joan ducked away, Daddy quickly stepped forward, laying a conciliatory hand on Aunt Lou's arm. "Now, now, no one's making trouble. We're just trying to get to the bottom of this mess." He slid an arm around Kiki, pulling her snugly next to him.

One of the deputies eased into the dining room, picking up and pocketing a napkin.

Aunt Lou ran a hand over her face. "I don't understand. Everything was fine this morning. That fire has somehow opened a gate to hell. Even my neighbors are turning against me!" She stamped a sensible Red Cross shoe. "All right. If you're going to look for my husband, I'm coming along." Her expression was grim. "Dinner is done."

Col. and Mrs. Moore exchanged glances. "Get your coats on, everyone," the colonel said. "We may as well turn this into a parade."

On the walk to the barn and outbuildings, Kiki stayed as far away from Aunt Lou as possible. Sheriff Madding got to the barn first. When he touched the heavy latch, there was frantic barking from inside.

Col. Moore turned to Aunt Lou. "You got an unhappy pooch there—doesn't get locked up much, I guess."

Aunt Lou hesitated. "Harry likes to have the dog with him." She frowned. "Where did he go that he wouldn't take Sparky?"

"Did he know you were having company?" Madding asked.

"He invited them, Sheriff. He told me they were coming for dinner and then didn't say another word. I was fit to be tied—I wanted to hear what was going on next door!" Her eyes shifted to glance at the girls. "But he was in a mood—I haven't seen him so upset in a long time. I know better than to bother him when he's like that."

The barking had turned into howling. One of the deputies gripped the door latch. "Okay to let him out?"

Aunt Lou inclined her chin slightly. When the bolt slid back, Sparky nosed the doors apart and plunged through the opening, whining and wiggling. He circled the group, sniffing everyone's feet before falling in a panting heap next to Aunt Lou.

Joan knelt to stroke the dog's head. "Where's Uncle Harry, boy?" Sparky responded by licking her face.

The deputy chuckled, "That pooch is cuter than he is smart."

Madding moved away from the barn. "Let's do a quick check of the outbuildings." He nodded to his deputies. "Mrs. Partridge, if your husband's not here, where would he be? Is there some place he goes to unwind—Cactus Pete's or one of the bars downtown?"

"No. He's not a drinker. And he wouldn't be likely to miss supper—no, sir." Aunt Lou's voice was little more than a whisper.

The deputies came across the yard. "No sign of anyone, Sheriff."

"Well, then," Madding said, "let's check out the fire scene, for starters. He didn't get a firsthand look this afternoon; maybe that's where he is. Why don't you take the women back inside, Colonel Moore, in case Harry shows up in the next half hour or so? Searching the old building and grounds won't take long—you folks may as well finish that meal."

Daddy reached for the handle of his truck door. "We'll go with you, Madding. That's our property—I want to be around when you search it. Besides, Mrs. Partridge said she wants to help look for her husband." He turned to Aunt Lou. "Am I right on that?"

Aunt Lou nodded. Sheriff Madding grimaced, muttering some swear word Kiki didn't know. He stomped over to his own vehicle. "Okay, let's get this show on the road."

On the short ride home, Kiki perched on Joan's lap next to her parents. The close quarters of the truck cab felt warm and safe, cocoon-like. In the hour since they'd left home, a soupy mist had floated into the orchards, wrapping the trees with damp tendrils. Kiki wished they didn't have to leave the truck.

No one spoke while they rolled along the country road, following the sheriff's vehicle through the gathering darkness. All too soon, red brake lights flashed ahead of them; they were home. Col. Moores' truck nosed up against a corner of the old house.

The sheriff called, "Leave your lights on so we can see to look around."

Beyond the shadowy building, a darker shape moved. Kiki sat up straight. "Did you see that? Something's out there."

"It's too dark to see anything," Col. Moore said. "Run around back and switch on the yard light."

"You want to come with me, Joan?"

Joan shook her head, jumping down from the truck. Kiki jumped down, too, and, instead of following her father's orders, sauntered after her sister.

"Get a move on, Kiki! We need that light," the colonel snapped.

With a groan, Kiki darted around the building to the light switch.

At the back corner she reached for the wood siding, expecting to feel chipped paint. Instead, her fingers brushed against rough cloth. Suddenly a hand clamped against her throat and she was shoved against the wall. Something hit her stomach; she felt an excruciating pain, and her breath was knocked out of her. While she was bent double, a foul-tasting rag was jammed into her mouth and she was slung under a rough arm. When she stiffened, hoping to pull loose, her attacker snarled and shook her like a rag doll. She tried to kick—a skull-jarring slap put a stop to that.

"Damn brat!" came a hoarse whisper. She recognized the voice. It was Uncle Harry.

With Kiki over his shoulder, Harry took off running. Then, just about the time she thought her insides were going to come right out through the rag, he slowed to a walk and stopped. He threw her face down, hard, onto some slimy stones. Icy water and the stink of rotting plants went up her nose. They were at the creek.

She got her knees up under her, losing one shoe in the struggle. When she tucked her arms in, Harry put a boot in her back, shoving her flat. He squatted next to her.

"You're worse than a damned yellow jacket, buzzing around any rotten stuff you find. I can't take you with me—best I can do is hide you somewhere and hope to buy some time so I can get the hell away."

Harry sniffed, wiping his nose on his sleeve. "Why'd you have to go running back there, anyway? I was just saying one last goodbye before taking off. Wouldn't have to go at all if it wasn't for you, you nosy kid, bringing all this heartache to Lou and me."

Harry's hand cupped the back of her head, pressing hard. She blinked back tears. There was a gulping sound—was he crying?

"Poor old Lou; I always told her our girl would come back someday. She didn't need to know what really happened up there." His voice dropped to a whisper. "This whole can o' worms is your fault, you and that damn Herschfeldt. Hell,

I'm innocent as a babe."

He stared at Kiki. "Okay, I'll admit, I was glad June Bug had a boyfriend; I was sick of being odd man out with her and Lou."

He rolled his eyes under their shaggy brows. "I knew he was a mean sort, but who would've thought he'd up and kill her? He said it was a' accident. Damned if I know what happened; I wasn't even there. He come an' told me, then threatened to tell Lou if I didn't help him burn the place down. Then, after all that, the son of a bitch took off." A long sigh escaped his lips. "Now, because of you and your meddling, I gotta disappear just like he did!"

Kiki didn't dare move, even though her face was mashed into the stony creek bed. She felt a sob rising up in her throat; it took all her strength to swallow it. Harry stopped talking. She heard him moving around. She tried to get her brain to work—what was he doing?

After a moment he grabbed her wrists, twisted them behind her back and tied them with scratchy twine. His knee pressed on her spine, and he tied her ankles together, too. Now there was more than fear keeping her still.

Harry began muttering—curious, rhyming words. Oh, dear god, she thought. Is he saying a prayer?

She heard shuffling sounds—he was moving around—then rustling in the bushes to her right—a whispered, "Goddammit!" Silence.

Chapter Seventeen

It seemed like forever that Kiki lay there, too scared to move and barely breathing. She gradually became aware of a tinkling sound—water trickling through the rocks. Eventually, a frog croaked. When a mosquito landed on her exposed cheek, she squinted. One eyelid cracked open. Along the ground the light changed from black to translucent silver. She turned her shoulder a fraction, wincing in advance of the expected slap. It didn't happen. She pulled her knees up to her stomach, inching onto her side. A hopeful thought intruded: maybe he's gone.

Kiki stared into the darkness, trying to make out the foliage around her. She looked toward the silver light. It had shape. It looked just like Rosalie June. Am I dead, Kiki wondered?

The ghost stood quietly, looking down at Kiki. There was the softest of whispers, like a shushing breeze. "Mama won't be happy he did this. I'm telling."

The form dissolved. In her head, Kiki yelled, "Come back! Don't leave me here by myself!"

Suddenly furious at her helplessness, Kiki rubbed her mouth against the rocks. The gag wouldn't budge. She stretched her legs, rolled over, and pushed herself into a sitting position against a tree trunk. She tried to think: her wrists and ankles were burned raw from the twine, her head throbbed, and her shoulder hurt, bad. But I'm not dead, like Rosalie June, she realized. And I think he's gone.

The arm resting against the tree stump began to itch in an odd, crawly way. Something was walking on her skin. A scream got lost in the gag. Kiki jerked, tipping over. She rolled into the trickling water, hoping the bug, or bugs, would wash away. After a minute in the icy water, the itching stopped. She heaved herself back over onto the water's edge. She was very, very cold now. With agonized effort she wrenched herself around to sit up, legs against her chest. She leaned forward, resting her bruised face on her knees. Her thoughts went to her father. Would he think she ran away again? Would he be mad at her? Oh, Daddy, she whispered into the gag, please don't be mad. Please come and find me. If only she'd told him about the ghost!

A cricket chirped, very close by. Kiki jumped. She shook herself, thinking, a cricket—it's just a cricket. Get a grip.

She concentrated on the sounds around her: gurgling water, rustling leaves, a lone bullfrog somewhere down the creek. Within the groaning of tree branches she thought she heard something else. Yes, there it was again—a growl, like a truck's engine. Was Harry coming back to get her? She pulled herself into a tight ball, squeezing her eyes shut. The only prayer she knew was, "Now I lay me down to sleep, I pray the Lord my soul to keep." She focused on the words, one ear tuned to the rumble of the truck's engine. The noise stopped. A door thunked open. A dog whined.

Someone shouted, "Go get her, boy!"

There was a loud crash in the bushes. Kiki heard snuffling, close by. Something cold and wet nuzzled her ear. Tears formed behind her eyelids. Her mind said, "Help me, please, Doggie!"

A voice, not Uncle Harry's, yelled, "Over here, by the creek. He's found her!"

A large, muddy paw tapped her shoulder. Kiki opened one eye. Sparky was sitting next to her, his breath warm on her face.

A beam of light bounced through the brush. In the darkness behind it, she could just make out a man's shape. It was not Uncle Harry.

When the man knelt next to her, smelling of acrid anxiety and stale tobacco, Kiki squinted into Sheriff Madding's stubbled face. "Okay, kid. We're here now."

Another face, eerie behind the beam of a second flashlight, floated into her line of sight. Daddy.

"Kiki! You're alive! Thank God." Col. Moore traded places with the sheriff, squatting on the ground. He put his hand to her cheek, barely touching her.

While the sheriff talked into his two-way radio, the colonel's calloused fingers eased the gag from Kiki's mouth. When it came free, she gulped air for a second before emitting a hoarse, "Thanks."

Col. Moore used his knife to free her wrists and ankles. She heard him suck in his breath—the rope burns probably looked as bad as they felt—and he stared off into the trees before saying, in an odd, cracking voice, "Where else are you hurt? Can you move?"

Kiki nodded and felt a jolt of pain. When she swiped her wrist at a loose strand of hair, she smelled blood. Her stomach flip-flopped, and she gagged. She closed her eyes. "Did you catch him, Daddy?"

"Not yet, but we will. We damn sure will."

The sheriff walked over, carrying a blanket. "Put this around her, Colonel, and then I need to ask her some questions. I'm sorry, but I have to."

Col. Moore tucked the blanket carefully around Kiki, cradling her head on his arm. "Go ahead, Sheriff. She can handle it. She's tough; she's a Moore." There was pride in his voice.

Madding knelt by them. "How you doin', kid?" The Halloween grimace on his face was, most likely, his idea of a reassuring smile. "Can you stand up?"

Kiki got to her knees and reached for her father. He lifted her as delicately as if she was a porcelain figurine. When her feet touched dirt, she looked down. "Hey, I'm missing a shoe."

"Yeah," Col. Moore said. "That's how we found you. I'll tell you that story later. Right now you have to tell the sheriff what happened—who did this. Can you do that?"

Kiki looked at the sheriff, surprised. Didn't he know it

was Uncle Harry? She opened her sore, cracked lips and the words tumbled out: "When I went around to turn on the backyard light, Uncle Harry grabbed me. He stuffed that rag in my mouth so I couldn't yell. Then he put me over his shoulder and took off. It seemed like he ran for a long time, 'til we got to the creek." She started to cry again. "After he tied me up, he kicked my head and stomped on me."

"How long ago did he leave?" Madding bit off each word.

"I don't know." Her voice trailed off. She wiped her eyes on the back of a bloody hand. "I don't know how long it was. Sorry."

The colonel leaned in, brushing her hair back in a rare, comforting gesture. Sheriff Madding went over to his truck and started talking on his two-way radio. Kiki didn't know exactly what an APB was, but it sounded serious. When he was finished, Madding lifted his hat and smoothed back his thinning hair.

"My men are on the way, Colonel. I'll wait here for them. Take your daughter home—you can use my truck. I'll send the medics to your house." Madding glanced at Kiki with an oddly embarrassed expression.

Col. Moore cradled Kiki in his arms, turning his face away. In the quietest tone she had ever heard from him, he said, "Did he do anything else, kid? I mean, did he, er, touch you anywhere he shouldn't have? Did he force himself on you?"

He looked down at her clothes, which, although muddy and torn, were still wrapped around her.

Kiki blushed. "You mean, rape, Daddy? Like Mama told us about? No. He just kicked the dickens out of me. He was real mad. Kept saying everything was my fault—me and Herschfeldt." She lay back against her father's shoulder, feeling unbearably weak and cold—so cold. She closed her eyes.

The sheriff put a hand on Col. Moore's shoulder. "Let's lock arms and carry her between us to the truck."

That short distance seemed to take forever. Every step jolted Kiki's aching body. She clenched her teeth to keep from wimpering.

On the bumpy ride across the orchard Sparky lay on the floor of the truck, chin resting on Kiki's foot. Col. Moore kept one eye on his daughter and one on the path through the trees. He gripped the steering wheel so hard his knuckles were white. "Just a little farther, Honey. We're almost there."

Kiki put a tentative hand on her father's arm. "I'm sorry for all this trouble, Daddy, right when you're getting ready to go overseas."

He stared out the windshield, opened his mouth to say something and closed it. They rode in silence. The ride smoothed out; they had found the paved road. They were almost home.

"I don't want any more talk of you being sorry. You didn't do anything wrong. If your mother and I had listened to you sooner, things wouldn't have gotten so bad."

Kiki couldn't believe her ears—Daddy, apologizing? "That's okay."

After a moment he said, "It's gonna be pretty hectic back at the house. Before we get there I want to tell you something, just between you and me." The dim light of the truck cab showed deep worry lines on his face. "It's time you learned a little more about your old dad."

They pulled up in front of the Moores' cottage. Sparky sat up, ears cocked. Moore put a calming hand on the dog's head, took a cigar stub out of his pocket and stuck it in his mouth.

"You know how you see ghosts?" He raised an eyebrow in question.

Kiki froze. "How'd you know about that? Did Joan blab? What a rotten big sister she is—always trying to get me in trouble!"

"Did I tell you it was okay to interrupt?"

She snapped her bloody lips shut.

"I got it from the horse's mouth—from the ghost you saw." He took the cigar from his mouth and rolled it between his thumb and forefinger, a tired frown pulling at his sunburned face. "Something I never thought I'd have to tell you: back when I was a teen-ager, still wet behind the ears, my old man beat me up so bad he almost killed me." His eyes flicked toward Kiki. "You wanna know why?"

She nodded, eyes wide.

"I started seeing people who were supposed to be dead. Pops thought I was making it up to get attention. I got attention all right; I still have the scars on my back from that beating."

He shifted in his seat, looking nervous. "So, you see, I have that curse—if you want to call it that—just like you. Don't spread it around. The world isn't exactly ready for people like you and me."

Kiki stared. She was speechless.

He chewed on the slimy green cigar, pointing toward the blackness they'd just driven through. "That damn ghost appeared when I was over by the barbecue pit, looking for you. The sheriff and his men were just a few feet away, but they didn't see it. Sparky growled when she showed up—maybe he saw her." Col. Moore sighed. "You're lucky. If she hadn't gotten my attention we would've just thought you ran away again. We were about to quit looking for you."

The breath Kiki had been holding came out in a whoosh. "You saw Rosalie June? You saw the ghost?"

He nodded. "Yeah—it surprised the hell out of me. I had no idea we had a ghost here. When she handed me your shoe and told me to fetch you down by the creek, I damn near dropped my teeth."

Col. Moore looked over to the light streaming out of the house's open front door. He turned to Kiki. "That ghost said, 'Don't let him get away with it this time.' What did she mean?"

Kiki's battered brain tried to form a response. The starch in her spine was long gone; she stayed erect, just barely, eyes glued to her father's agonized expression.

"It's a long story, Daddy. Do we have to talk about it right now?"

He sighed. "Just a little, babe—the sheriff needs something to go on."

She pushed the hair away from her eyes, leaning into his shoulder. "That ghost was Aunt Lou and Uncle Harry's daughter. She died in the old house. The man who lived there—he was her boyfriend—he did it, and Uncle Harry knew. They didn't tell anyone, not even Aunt Lou." Kiki's voice dropped to a barely audible whisper. She flicked her eyes away from her father's stunned face. "I think that's why she's still here. She wants her mother to know how she died."

Col. Moore gulped, stubbed his cigar into the ashtray, and gave Kiki a searching look. "And you just stumbled into this old cesspool?"

She responded with the ghost of a grin. "Yes, sir, pretty much. I guess, when I found the skeleton and those rags, Uncle Harry got worried. Maybe he thought Aunt Lou would find out."

"Jesus," Col. Moore breathed. "Partridge was in on the death of his own child?" He blinked. "He's been punishing himself, carrying this around, all these years—must've gone over the edge years ago."

When Col. Moore climbed out of the truck, he hurried around to the passenger side, reaching in for Kiki. He gave her a sad little smile. "That story I told you doesn't leave this truck Understand?"

Kiki crossed her heart, nodding.

On the short trip from the truck to the house, Kiki recalled Mama's comment about Daddy being a natural dancer—graceful and strong. He carried his injured daughter easily and carefully, as if she weighed nothing and was very precious. When they reached the sofa, he eased her down on the cushions. Mama hovered nearby, fear and shock radiating from her.

"I'm okay, Mama, just a little bloody," Kiki croaked.

Across the room Joan cowered, looking terrified.

Chapter Eighteen

"Come on, now, gals. Help me get her settled." Col. Moore's voice cracked.

"Do you want a wet washcloth, Emily? Let's get the mud off her face." Isabel Barret's tremulous voice came from the kitchen doorway, where she stood next to Aunt Lou. While tears rolled down Mrs. Barret's face, Aunt Lou looked calm—almost bored.

Mrs. Moore nodded, murmuring, "She needs to go to the hospital, Bill."

"Sheriff's got a medic on the way, Emily. Be here any minute." And then, louder, the colonel said, "Get another blanket, Joan—she's in shock."

Someone tucked a quilt around Kiki. When a rough cloth brushed her cheek, she moaned, "No, no. Don't touch me!"

Mrs. Moore whispered, "Just a little, honey."

The cloth brought with it a soothing trickle of clean water. Kiki relaxed, drifting again into half-consciousness. Sometime later, she opened her eyes to see Sheriff Madding standing near her father. "Sheriff," Kiki croaked, "did you tell Aunt Lou?"

Col. Moore must have heard. He looked at Madding, jerking his chin toward the kitchen, and the two men left the room.

When Kiki tried to stretch her numb legs, a tidal wave of pain flipped her stomach—she upchucked and began to cry. Everyone in the room, except Aunt Lou, rushed to her side.

"Let me help, Mama." Joan leaned over, her warm breath in Kiki's ear. As she sponged off her sister's face, she whispered, "Should I show them what you found, kid? You know, the stuff that belonged to that girl?"

Kiki blinked, shaking her head. Her glance drifted to the mirror across the room, where Aunt Lou was reflected with a shadowy form leaning against her—Rosalie June. Kiki gasped and tried to sit up, but Aunt Lou's angry voice brought a wave of nausea and she slumped back into the pillows.

"She found something of my daughter's? When were you going to tell me about this?"

Emily Moore hobbled across the carpet to stand in front of Aunt Lou. "Please go into the kitchen, Lou. Kiki needs our full attention right now. We'll deal with those other issues later."

"No! How dare you put the whims of that errant girl ahead of me? Spare the rod and spoil the child, I always say!"

From behind her mother's skirt, Kiki could see Aunt Lou's face, radiating fury. She prayed the woman wouldn't hit her mother.

"Hush, Lou!" Mrs. Moore's usually soft voice was sharp, and her hands were balled into fists. She stood bigger than life, like a mother cat with its fur fluffed out.

Aunt Lou turned absolutely white. "I will not hush! I want to know what she's found. I'm tired of all these ugly secrets."

The kitchen door opened; Sheriff Madding leaned into the room. "Mrs. Partridge, you need to come in here. Ma'am." Although his words were courteous, his tone was firm.

Aunt Lou turned, put a finger against his chest, and said, "What's going on here? Get back out there and look for Harry!"

Sheriff Madding recoiled; just then a siren sounded in the distance.

"Bill," Emily Moore called. "It's the ambulance!"

Col. Moore stepped in from the kitchen. "Can my wife ride along with Kiki, Sheriff? I want to stay here until you pick up ..." He looked at Aunt Lou. "... Partridge."

A draft blew in from the kitchen. Mrs. Barret, moving over to shut the door, jumped back and bumped the sheriff. Startled, he looked at her and then into the kitchen.

"God Almighty," he yelled. His hand went to his holstered revolver.

Uncle Harry stood just beyond the door frame, his gray skin and hollow-eyed stare giving him the look of an upright corpse. Wisps of hair protruding from an old knit cap were a feeble reminder of the robust old man who'd left the Moores' ranch just a few hours earlier.

"That sure ain't me, Sheriff."

For a second no one moved, then the room erupted. Mama lurched forward to shield Kiki, someone shouted, and both Col. Moore and the sheriff tackled Harry.

Aunt Lou, yelling, "Hey! That's my husband!" grabbed a fistful of Col. Moore's shirt.

Sheriff Madding pushed Harry against the wall, elbowing the colonel away. "Back off, Moore! I'll handle this."

One of the deputies grabbed Col. Moore's shoulder, gun drawn. Moore moved back a step.

Mrs. Barret sang out, "The ambulance is here!"

A siren yelped and was quiet. Metal doors slammed; footsteps pounded on the front steps, and the front door swung open. Four stretcher-bearing medics bustled in, stopping at the sight of the deputies' guns. Then the pink-cheeked medic in the lead spotted Kiki and barked, "Comin' through, folks. Clear a path."

Madding shouted, "All right, everyone, at ease. Let's get the girl into the ambulance, then move Partridge out. "

"Oh, no, you don't! Release my husband this instant!" Aunt Lou pushed forward.

The sheriff, distracted, loosened his grip and Harry jerked around, taking a step toward the front door.

Emily Moore screamed, "Watch out! He's getting away!"

Sheriff Madding lurched forward, twisting the old man's arms behind him. There was the click of handcuffs, and Harry was pushed against the wall.

Kiki felt a touch on her shoulder; she looked into the

smiling face of one of the ambulance men. "We're puttin' you on the stretcher, kid. Lay still and let us do the work."

Aunt Lou, hovering near Harry, ran a hand across her face as if confused. Col. Moore spoke to her. "Do you feel a chill, Lou?"

He caught Kiki's eye. She nodded. The ghost was still there, next to Aunt Lou.

A medic intoned, "Let's keep that back and neck straight."

Mrs. Barret, who must have been listening to Daddy, broke in, "I sure did!" Her face showed sudden understanding. "Oh, my. Is it what I think it is, Colonel? Is the ghost here?"

No one answered.

One of the medics said, "Think we should give her a shot, Sam?"

"No, not 'til we know if there's a concussion."

Harry spoke up. "Can I apologize before they haul the kid away?"

"Don't you get anywhere near her," Col. Moore growled. "You think 'sorry' will fix everything, bring your own child back to life?"

The face Harry turned to Daddy could have been carved from stone.

The medic's voice rattled in the tinny silence. "Okay— one, two, three, lift." In one agonizing lurch, Kiki was on the stretcher.

Aunt Lou stared at Harry. "What's this about Rosalie June and a ghost? Has everyone gone crazy?"

Col. Moore spoke. "Ask him who the skeleton was, Lou. It was small—about the size of a teen-aged girl. And it dates back to when your daughter disappeared." He turned a grim face to Harry. "Why the hell didn't you tell her a long time ago?"

The old man's face twisted into a terrible grimace. "I've been keeping that filthy secret all these years, protecting that

142

woman, and look where it got me—hog-tied!" A coughing fit engulfed him.

Aunt Lou shuddered. "She's dead? My Rosalie June's dead—that can't be. She ran away. You said so, Harry!"

Her voice trailed off, then came out again in a querulous whine. "How could she be the thing you found in that attic? She never went up there. That was Mr. Herschfeldt's bedroom … Oh, my god!"

Aunt Lou staggered toward her husband, arms outstretched. He turned away.

From the stretcher, Kiki called out, "You have to believe it, Aunt Lou. Please, please believe it so the bad stuff will end."

Col. Moore brushed a hand across his eyes. "She's right, Lou. Whether you want to face it or not, your daughter died in that bedroom and Harry knew about it."

Emily Moore spoke, expressing fear and awe. "All the awful things happening here—are they part of this mess? Could that be, Bill?"

The colonel nodded, eyes on Aunt Lou. "She was a pretty girl; had curly red hair. I guess you or Harry had red hair once, Lou?"

Kiki felt a shiver travel up from her toes. "Please, Aunt Lou, say you believe she died up there. She needs to hear that from her mother!" With an effort, she focused her eyes on the old woman. "Please, Aunt Lou. When Daddy goes overseas, Joan and Mama and I have to live here by ourselves."

The front door, standing open for the stretcher, creaked. "Hey! Was that the wind?" The medic sounded scared.

Harry sneered. "You shoulda let the place burn down. That woulda got rid of any pesky haunting. Fire gets rid of everything."

Rosalie June, still hovering near Aunt Lou, turned toward her father. Kiki felt the room's temperature drop.

"Partridge, if I were you I'd shut up, now." Sheriff Madding spit out the words. "You're under arrest."

Col. Moore leaned into Harry's face. "You idiot, your daughter's right here with us, and she's mad as hell."

Harry shook his head. "You must be shell-shocked, Colonel. You've lost your marbles."

Rosalie June drifted through the cluster of people, trailing cold shivers. As Kiki watched, light flowed out of each person and into the ghost. The pallor in Rosalie June's cheeks was replaced by a rosy glow.

Col. Moore stepped over to the stretcher, taking Kiki's hand.

Mrs. Barret thumped her fist on the arm of a chair. "Harry, for God's sake, tell Lou what happened. Now!"

Harry jumped like he'd been poked with a cattle prod. "All, right, dammit. It was a' accident. Herschfeldt roughed her up and went too far. Then he ran off and left me holdin' the bag."

Sheriff Madding turned to one of his deputies. "Get out your notepad, Junior. It's gonna be a long night."

"My baby," Aunt Lou whispered. "She died—suffered, and no one told me."

As Kiki and Daddy watched, Rosalie June stepped in front of Harry. Placing her hands around his neck, she squeezed. His eyes bulged; his mouth opened, but no sound came out. He grabbed at the air around his throat. Then, tongue protruding through age-stained teeth, he sank to his knees. The ghost went down on her knees also, maintaining her grip on his wrinkled neck.

The deputy closest to Harry watched him slump to the floor, puzzled. "Whatcha doin' there, fella?"

The old man shuddered, collapsed. His body went limp. A sort of shadow-Harry stood up, looked around, and walked away. Rosalie June drifted over to Aunt Lou, placing ethereal arms around her mother.

"Thank you, Mama," could have been a whispering air

current. Then, just ahead of Kiki's stretcher, the ghost of Rosalie June drifted out of the house and down the steps. The outdoor air claimed her.

Sheriff Madding knelt next to Harry. "What the hell? He's not breathing!" He looked up at one of the medics. "Get over here, will ya? This man's not lookin' so good."

"Let's go, boys."

Kiki's stretcher moved through the front door and down the steps. She reached for her father's hand. "She killed him, didn't she?"

"Yeah. She took care of her unfinished business."

Just before the ambulance doors slammed shut, Kiki got a look at the old house. It still looked abandoned, old and rotting. But it didn't look haunted, anymore.

The End

Made in the USA
San Bernardino, CA
14 November 2014